TO HAVE AND TO HOLD

Tragedy had taken its toll on Hannah Cullen's family and she had been left to care for her younger sister and two brothers. Hannah was determined to make a life for herself and her siblings, but her road to happiness was to be a bumpy one. Firstly, she was unfairly dismissed from her job. Then, when she went down to the dock to meet her friend Christian, a handsome Danish fisherman, she saw him arm in arm with another woman . . .

SYLVIA BROADY

TO HAVE AND TO HOLD

Complete and Unabridged

LINFORD
Leicester

First published in Great Britain in 2002

First Linford Edition
published 2003

British Library CIP Data

Broady, Sylvia
    To have and to hold.—Large print ed.—
Linford romance library
    1. Love stories
    2. Large type books
    I. Title
    823.9'2 [F]

ISBN 0–7089–4977–0

Published by
F. A. Thorpe (Publishing)
Anstey, Leicestershire

Set by Words & Graphics Ltd.
Anstey, Leicestershire
Printed and bound in Great Britain by
T. J. International Ltd., Padstow, Cornwall

This book is printed on acid-free paper

1

The year was 1868, and, with a determined spring in her step, Hannah Cullen walked down Princes Street. Waiting for a hansom cab to pass before crossing the road, she gazed up at the brilliant blue sky. It was a perfect, autumn day, one matching her mood of optimism. Carefully lifting up the skirt of her best grey wollen dress to avoid the soggy leaves scattered in the gutter, she crossed over. Pacing her eagerness, she made her way towards Arden Square and hopefully to her new future.

A sudden tear sprang into her dark brown eyes as she recalled the untimely death of her parents — her father lost at sea and her dear mother from consumption, which had resulted in her and her young siblings being placed in an orphanage. On that most terrible, frightening day, she made a vow to reunite her sister and two brothers and provide a home for them. Edward Smith-Allen, a trustee of the orphanage, who initiated the move to the orphanage, was the man, for some unknown reason to Hannah, to whom her mother entrusted the welfare of her sorrowing children.

On reaching Arden Square, Hannah stopped, her eyes lighting up admiringly at the neat houses, their well-scrubbed steps leading up to tastefully-painted, wooden doors, windows bright and shiny. She breathed in the sweet-smelling air that only carried the faintest whiff of fish from the distant Humber Dock of the port of Kingston-upon-Hull, near to her temporary lodgings.

The rumbling of a horse and cart mingled with the shout of a news-seller as she paused to read the newspaper placard. It announced that Edward, the Prince of Wales, would officially open the new dock now under construction in July 1869. She wondered if he would bring his wife, the beautiful Danish princess. Immediately she thought of Christian Hansen, the tall, blond, handsome Danish fisherman and her heart quivered. But then just as quickly she banished him from her thoughts.

Hannah stopped outside 27 Arden Square, her destination. She stared in dismay at the unwashed steps, the discarded rubbish strewn about in the basement area and her heart sank. Visibly she shrunk back, the skin of her creamy complexion wrinkling in disgust, but swiftly she told herself to be positive. Holding her head high, she tucked a wayward strand of chestnut coloured hair beneath her plain black hat and squared her shoulders.

Ready to meet any challenge, she mounted the steps. Raising the green-moulded knocker, she gave a polite tap and let it fall. The sound echoed behind the door. She waited, but no one came in answer, so she knocked louder. From inside she heard the plaintive cry of a child, someone shouting and a scurry of feet. Then the door was wrenched open to reveal a flustered-looking, young woman with untidy brown hair flopping about her face, wearing a black dress and a grubby white apron.

'I've come in answer to the advertisement for the position of housekeeper,' Hannah stated clearly, but the woman didn't seem to be listening, her attention being distracted by the wailing of a child.

'Come in,' the woman gabbled, and promptly hurried up the staircase leaving Hannah alone in the dimly-lit hall.

As Hannah glanced about, dust was very much in evidence, covering the ornate mahogany hallstand and the two tall-backed chairs. Her nose twitched, smelling the neglect of the whole house. Her gaze travelled up the unpolished staircase as the cry of the child persisted. Suddenly the anxious face of a girl of about sixteen peered at her from over the banister at the top of the stairs.

'Can you come up, please, miss?'

Hannah followed the nursemaid into the nursery where the woman who had answered the door was trying to pacify a baby girl of about seven months who lay kicking in her crib. The woman, unable to calm the baby, flounced from the room without a word.

Hannah kneeled by the side of the crib of the distressed baby. Her little puckered face was red and she was holding her breath. On seeing Hannah, she let out a high-pitched scream then rammed her tiny fist into her mouth.

'You poor angel, it's them nasty teeth,' Hannah soothed.

She lifted the wrestling baby from the crib, holding her securely.

'There, there,' she soothed, then easing the struggling child over her shoulder, she gently patted her back.

Mercifully the child's cry lessened and Hannah turned to address the nursemaid, who looked half asleep.

'What's the child's name?'

'Charlotte, miss.'

'Have you a child's cooling powder?'

'I don't know, miss. I can go and ask Ruby,' she said and hurried from the nursery.

Hannah walked to and fro. Whenever she stopped, Charlotte started to cry again.

'Where's your mama?' she asked softly, hugging the child close.

The nursemaid returned with a cooling powder.

'What are you going to do, miss?'

'You undo the packet, taking care not to spill it, crease the underneath of the paper down the middle, long ways. I'll open Charlotte's mouth wide and you let the powder slide in. Ready?'

Charlotte struggled, but not one grain of powder was lost. Then, after the baby had been fed and made comfortable, Hannah cradled the sleepy bundle in her arms before laying her back in the crib. Then she turned to the nursemaid.

'At last!' she exclaimed, but the girl was fast asleep, her head lolling on the back of the low chair where she had slumped.

Checking again to make sure the sleeping baby was all right, Hannah went downstairs to find Ruby. She found her in the basement kitchen and the two women hugged each other.

'I thought it would be you,' Hannah said, 'my dear friend from the orphanage.'

Standing back, she viewed Ruby.

'But you're much thinner.'

'You would be, working here. There aren't enough hours in the day or night to do everything.'

Hannah sat on a low stool opposite her friend.

'But what about other staff?'

'There's only me and Jenny, the nursemaid, and a washerwoman who comes in twice a week.'

'What about the present house-keeper?'

'Her, the old bag? She got the push last week for pinching. She even took the baby's food, I ask you. What kind of person does that?'

'And what did the mistress say?' Hannah enquired, thinking of Mrs Smith-Allen, her former employer, who had her dismissed because she dared to complain about the indecent behaviour of their nephew.

'There isn't one. Poor lady died after the bairn was born,' Ruby replied.

'Oh, dear, how sad. No wonder Charlotte is fretting,' she said sympathetically. 'Do you know who I am supposed to see about the housekeeper's position?'

'An aunt of Mr Burnett's was supposed to come, but she sent a note to say she's indisposed. You best wait and see the master. He's usually home by six.'

'Anyone else applied?'

'Some woman came by, but she soon hopped it when Charlotte started to wail.'

Ruby leaned forward to rake the ebbing fire, rekindling it with logs and coals from the fireside basket.

'The house is in a bit of a state,' she said. 'Every time I start to do something, the bairn cries. Jenny's up through the night with her, so she's too tired during the day.'

She swung the iron kettle across the fanning flames of the fire.

'We'll have a pot of tea.'

Leaning back in her chair, she closed her eyes. Hannah looked round the kitchen. The stone sink was full of greasy crockery and cutlery, with vegetable peelings scattered on a chopping board.

'Have you a spare apron, Ruby?'

'Aye, top drawer of dresser,' she replied, not opening her eyes. 'Laundry woman's reliable.'

The apron swamped Hannah's slender figure, but she hitched it up and tied it securely round her waist and pushed up the sleeves of her dress.

'I'll tidy up.'

Ruby watched her through half-closed eyes.

'I hope you get the job, Hannah. This

house needs a good organiser.'

With everything eventually washed and put away, surfaces scrubbed, floor swept, tea brewing, Hannah gave her sleeping friend a gentle nudge.

'Ready for you, Ruby.'

Ruby sat up with a start.

'I was just resting me eyes. You pour, Hannah. I'll just look at the master's dinner. It's only hot pot. I'm not much of a cook, but he doesn't grumble.'

While enjoying a cup of tea, they caught up on events since the time they'd both left the orphanage.

'I came here about a year ago,' Ruby said. 'I started as kitchen maid then the old cook retired and I took over. Now what about you? I thought you'd struck lucky, companion to Mrs Smith-Allen's niece.'

Hannah felt her face flush and a slight panic rise within her. She took a sip of tea, calming herself before she spoke.

'It was the nephew actually, but he was rather careless where he put his hands and I complained about him to Mrs Smith-Allen who didn't believe me. She had me dismissed immediately.'

She lowered her eyes from Ruby's glare, shuddering inwardly, feeling once again the uninvited creepy touch of Winthrop Huntington.

'I would have given him what for,' Ruby said bluntly. 'Why didn't you tell Mr Smith-Allen?'

'He was away in London.'

'What about a reference for this job?'

Her composure regained, Hannah gave a faint smile.

'I will have to go and see Mr Smith-Allen about that. I think he will be sympathetic towards me because he kindly sent me money for my lodgings and to buy this new dress. His note said it was my salary owing to me from the fourteen months I worked in his employment.'

Rising from the stool, Hannah said, 'Ruby, do you mind if I go upstairs? I can make myself useful and keep an eye on baby then Jenny can come down to have her tea.'

'By, heck, you're wicked,' Ruby remarked admiringly.

Upstairs, Hannah moved quietly about the nursery, collecting the baby's soiled garments and folding away fresh linen. She sang softly. Replenishing the fire and securing the guard, she sat down on the nursing chair and listened to the gentle breathing of the sleeping child.

It was so peaceful here, and she felt at home in this pleasant room, tastefully decorated in colours of soft grey and primrose yellow. It was obvious that a lot of love and care had gone into making it lovely, and so sad that little Charlotte's mother had died.

The child murmured, tossing, flinging out a chubby arm. Hannah leaned forward in her chair and slipped a finger into the curled palm of the baby's hand, and for some reason, Christian Hansen's face flickered across her mind's eye.

Over the past weeks, she had tried not to think of him because it upset her too much. She had thought him her true friend, one whom she could rely on when in difficulty. When she worked for the Smith-Allens he had visited her when home from his fishing trips and they spent some happy times together, walking out. But sadly his shore leave, usually only two or three days, didn't always coincide with her one in three Sunday afternoons off so consequently they didn't meet as often as they wished.

When she was dismissed from her job, she hadn't seen Christian for months, but he was the first person she turned to. She closed her eyes, recalling the day when she had gone down to the dock.

A mischievous wind had raced in from the North Sea, whistling and rattling down the Humber, cutting cross the dock, tugging devilishly at Hannah's skirt. She clambered over damaged fishing nets and sails, scouring the vessels in dock looking for the Saint Beaut, the fishing smack on which Christian Hansen sailed. But it was nowhere to be seen.

Wildly, she looked around seeking someone to ask about its whereabouts and when it was due home. Foot-weary from her trek from the Smith-Allens' house in Albion Street, she made her way to the shed where the daily fish market was held. Now late afternoon, it was almost deserted, its fish packed in ice on its way by railroad to destinations as near as the West Riding and as far away as London.

At the entrance to the shed, seated on an upturned crate, was Jonas, an old seadog, repairing nets. Hunched over his work, his gnarled but experienced fingers deftly manoeuvred the crude needle. As she approached, he looked up, shading his eyes against the sunlight, questioning. She didn't look like the usual women who frequented the dock. He waited for her to speak.

'Excuse me, please, do you know

when the Saint Beaut is due in?'

Jonas's curiosity was aroused.

'Be someone from your own family on it?' he asked.

A shyness crept over her as she replied.

'He's almost family. His name is Christian Hansen.'

'Danish lad?'

'You know him?'

'Aye, seen him a time or two.'

Jonas turned to gaze towards his beloved sea. Yes, he'd seen him and the lass who came to meet him. He swung round.

'You're in luck. Word is the Saint Beaut is about to enter the Humber.'

He saw the joy on her face as her eyes lit up and sparkled.

'Thank you. May I wait here until it comes in?'

'Aye, lass. Take a rest on them nets. They're dry,' he said indicating a pile of nets waiting repair.

Slipping down, she nestled her face against the coarseness of the braiding and breathed in the strong, lingering smell of fish and the salt of the sea. She felt strangely comforted.

She must have drifted off to sleep for the next thing she remembered was being gently nudged by Jonas.

'Saint Beaut in the lock,' he said.

Startled, she scrambled to her feet, pushing back her ruffled hair. She gratefully accepted a mug of steaming tea from him. The hot liquid revived her and brushing dust and bits of twine off her skirt, she moved nearer to the quayside. Darkness was falling as the fishing smack sailed into the dock, buffeting against the quay supports as its crew brought it to berth skilfully.

Hannah did a jig as excitement gripped her. She stood on the fringe of the small group of women and children waiting for their menfolk. A couple of women gave her sideways glances. She was a stranger and they must be wondering who she was. She wanted to shout out that she was Christian's woman here to welcome him home.

Then she heard the revelation of her inner voice — Christian's the man I love! She rejoiced, but it was to be cruelly cut short.

The first crewmen came ashore. Hannah watched them heading for the nearest beerhouse followed by their womenfolk and children.

Turning back to the smack, she saw Christian. The dim light of the boat's lantern shone on his blond hair and her heart did a double somersault. He looked taller, his face weathered to a golden shade, so handsome, she thought. Swinging his bag over his shoulder, he jumped ashore. Passion for him swept through her body up to her throat.

'Christian,' she called, but her voice was too soft and was carried away on the evening breeze.

He didn't see or hear her, but turned to kiss a young, dark-haired woman who'd linked her arm through his. They both laughed, as they walked away together. Hannah couldn't move. She stood alone on the quayside. Suddenly a gust of wind howled across the dock, bringing rain, hard and pelting, beating on her face and soaking her clothes.

Still she remained oblivious to the change in the weather only conscious of the image of Christian kissing another woman, until a hand touched her sodden shoulder and a voice croaked, 'Time to go home, lass. This isn't a safe place to hang around.'

Suddenly, Jenny's voice broke into Hannah's dreaming.

'The master's home. He's asking to see you.'

Downstairs, she tapped on the door of Mr Burnett's study. He opened it himself. A man of medium height, dark-brown hair and side whiskers, his eyes held Hannah's attention, dark-brown, like his hair, but so sad looking. A pang of sorrow touched her heart, but the proud tilt of his head pulled her up sharp. He wouldn't want sympathy from a stranger.

She smiled and said politely, 'Good

evening, sir. I'm Hannah Cullen. I've come in answer to your advertisement for the position of housekeeper.'

'Come in, Miss Cullen. Please, take a seat.'

She felt a sense of pride at being referred to as Miss Cullen. It made her feel worthy of herself. She sat opposite him on a high-back chair and folding her hands in her lap, she gave him her full attention.

'I understand you have met my daughter, Charlotte.'

His voice was deep, caring.

'Yes, sir.'

'What do you think of her?'

'She's a sweet child.'

'So like her mother,' he replied wistfully, then briskly he said, 'How old are you, Miss Cullen?'

She sat up straighter as if to make her look taller.

'I'm eighteen, sir.'

'Rather young for the position of housekeeper. What experience have you had?'

19

She jutted out her chin.

'I managed the house for my mother until she passed away. Looked after my two brothers and sister, and a lodger.'

She then described her life and work at the orphanage, and in the Smith-Allen household, telling him the truth about why she was dismissed.

'Good gracious, how terrible for you. Miss Cullen, I can reassure you, that sort of behaviour will not be tolerated here.'

She was conscious of him looking directly into her eyes and she knew instinctively that she could trust this man.

'Thank you, sir.'

'Good. Now, about the duties and responsibilities of housekeeper. I expect trustworthiness at all times. You will see to the household accounts, to be inspected weekly, marketing, menus, give guidance to cook, take care of linen, the cleaning duties. They have been neglected of late.'

He paused for breath and looked into

20

her honest eyes.

'The most important duty, however, is to oversee the care of my daughter. I understand you have already proved yourself in that direction.'

Hannah blushed.

'It seemed the natural thing to do.'

'You will find that my requirements are not too demanding. I rise at seven, breakfast at seven-thirty. I arrive home in the evening about six and spend an hour with Charlotte. I dine at eight, unless I go to my club. I expect my clothes to be brushed and clean linen laid out each day.'

Hannah nodded, thinking what an orderly life he led, and, as if he read her mind, he said, 'I'm afraid I am a creature of habit. My late wife insisted a well-run household must have a daily routine.'

Then a twinkle appeared in his sad-looking eyes, lighting them.

'Though I am not adverse to a pleasant diversion.'

He rose to his feet. Hannah rose also,

her fingers crossed behind her back.

'Miss Cullen, I formally offer you the position of housekeeper.'

Without hesitation she replied, 'And I accept, sir.'

'Done. Now I expect you to start immediately. Would your affairs allow that?'

'Yes, sir. I can go to my lodgings and collect my belongings and return within the hour.'

'Excellent.'

With the shadow of her past receding, Hannah soon settled into the routine at Arden Square. It therefore came as a surprise when she received a note from Mr Smith-Allen requesting her presence at his chambers. His groom, bringing with him the wicker basket containing the rest of her belongings, delivered the note.

'I wonder what he wants.'

She was puzzled as she and Ruby sorted the china cabinet together.

'I have to think about Georgie's and Lily's welfare. Mr Smith-Allen is still responsible for them. I'll ask Mr Burnett if I can go tomorrow afternoon.'

Ten minutes later, the china sorted, Hannah hurried from the kitchen. She wanted to have all the freshly-laundered curtains hung today. She loved this house, and was so happy here. She felt a glowing pride in the touches she'd administered. Earlier that morning she'd ventured into the overgrown garden at the back of the house and found hidden amidst a tangle of tall grasses a rose bush full of late, fragrant-perfumed roses. She couldn't resist picking the delicate pink blooms, enriched with shiny green leaves.

Robert Burnett seemed to appreciate her feminine touch, though he never said so, but she could tell. After his evening meal he would shut himself away in his study, surrounded by ledgers and books as he contemplated ways of improving his rundown business, a small printing press which he had inherited from his late father.

That night, as usual, Hannah knocked politely on his door before entering with a decanter of port. Setting the tray down on the wine table next to his chair, she coughed to attract his attention. He looked up from his ledger, pen poised. He seemed surprised to see her there.

'Please, sir,' she began.

He listened patiently to her request and her concern for her brother and sister still living in the orphanage.

'Of course you must go, Hannah. Mr Smith-Allen is a man of importance and by what you have told me, a most generous man.'

He pushed back the ledger.

'Enough of this. Sit down, Hannah, and take a glass of port with me.'

Astonished, Hannah replied, 'But, sir, I am but a servant.'

'This is my house, Hannah. Please take a seat.'

She sat on the very edge of the chair he indicated and sipped at the sweet red wine, letting it trickle down her throat, feeling its warmth. Relaxing, she listened to her employer. As he talked, mainly about Charlotte and snippets about his business, Hannah saw what a lonely man he was.

Next day, at two in the afternoon, Hannah presented herself at Mr Smith-Allen's chambers and was ushered immediately into his office. He rose to greet her.

'So good of you to come promptly, Hannah. Please, take a seat.'

Then for a few unguarded moments, Edward Smith-Allen allowed himself the pleasure to gaze upon Hannah, taking in the beautiful sheen of her chestnut hair, her well-defined bone structure and her creamy skin. Her mother would have been so proud of her.

She looked quite composed, except for her honey-brown eyes. They held a hint of apprehension. He felt saddened that his plan had gone astray and she was no longer living under his roof. But he must endeavour to maintain contact with her, no matter how slender. He smiled, wanting to reassure her that he still cared for her welfare, but it was difficult.

'Hannah, my dear girl, I'm sorry for the circumstances that forced you to leave my house. You are settled in your new position?'

'Yes, thank you, sir,' she replied politely.

'Should you require assistance on any matter, please don't hesitate to contact me here. I have not forgotten your mother's wishes.'

At the mention of her mother, Hannah lowered her gaze, a lump rising in her throat.

'Now to the business in hand,' he said, opening the report from the orphanage, 'the future of your sister, Lily. I understand from the matron that Lily has shown a tendency towards dressmaking. A suitable position has been found for her, with lodgings nearby. She is to leave at the end of the month. I have made arrangements for you to visit your sister, and you may also see your brother on Thursday week. Is that convenient for you?'

'Yes, sir.'

Fancy, she thought, Lily's thirteen, old enough for a proper job. She felt sure that Mr Burnett would grant her leave to visit.

'Any questions?'

'Yes, sir. What about our Georgie's future?'

'Georgie? He is receiving the same attention as the other boys, a thorough training in seamanship.'

'The sea?' Hannah said. 'Our Georgie doesn't like the sea,' she emphasised, jumping to her feet, her face flushed with indignation.

'Nonsense, girl. The sea's an admirable occupation. Your brother, Tom, thrives on it.'

'Yes, but Georgie is different.'

But he wasn't listening to her. He was looking at his pocket watch and without meeting her eyes said, 'You must excuse me. I have an important meeting to attend.'

Before she could voice further disapproval, a clerk entered and ushered her from the room. Out in the street, shaking with anger at Smith-Allen's patronising manner, she didn't notice the man across the road, waiting patiently.

'Hannah,' a voice said and a hand touched her shoulder lightly.

She turned slowly to gaze into the vivid blue eyes of Christian Hansen.

2

Her heart raced at the sight of him. Then remembering when she had last seen him, kissing another woman, she said coldly, 'Good afternoon, Christian. How are you?'

He stepped back to stare at her.

'I am well, Hannah, but why are you so formal?'

'Why indeed?' she retorted indignantly, unaware of people passing by and jolting against her.

Christian took hold of her arm to steer her to a quiet doorway.

'Hannah, we are friends, not enemies. Why are you acting this way?'

'You know very well.'

He frowned, puzzled.

'But I don't. You must explain.'

'I've no time. I'm expected back.'

'Ruby said it was all right for us to spend some time together.'

'Ruby? But how did you know where I'm working?'

'One of the crew off your Tom's smack told me. Hannah, please walk with me to the park.'

Her head and her heart began to battle. Her heart won. They walked in silence until reaching the park. Its trees were almost bare of leaves as they sat in the arbour, sheltered from the prevailing late autumn wind blowing off the Humber. She didn't really know what to say to Christian. They had been friends since childhood days when he first came to lodge at the family home just after her father died, and later visiting her when she was sent to the orphanage.

Once she began working, it became more difficult for their meetings to coincide with her time off and his home leave when the fishing smack was in port. And, she thought bitterly, he had found someone else. Hadn't she seen with her own eyes! Yet, in spite of that she couldn't deny he still held a special place in her heart. But did he feel the same way about her?

'Hannah, I have a gift for you,' Christian said softly.

Startled from her thoughts, she turned to look at him, surprised.

'I would have come sooner, but you didn't tell me of your move. Why not, Hannah?'

Tears filled her eyes, whether of sadness or regret she wasn't sure.

'I did come to see you. I waited for the Saint Beaut to berth, but you didn't see me as you were too busy paying attention to another woman.'

Angrily she jumped to her feet, tears coursing unheeded down her cheeks.

'I came to you for help, Christian Hansen.'

'Hannah!'

His arms were around her, comforting her. He drew her back down on the seat and let her sob. When she became quieter, he smoothed back her hair and gently, with the back of his hand, he wiped away her tears. Then lifting up her chin, he looked deep into her eyes.

'You should have come to my lodgings. The girl you saw me with is my landlady's daughter. She's just a friendly girl, nothing more to me.'

He sighed deeply. Then, wanting to lighten the atmosphere, he drew from the inside pocket of his jacket a small package wrapped in brown paper and handed it to her.

'For you, Hannah.'

By now all her anger and frustration had evaporated, leaving her feeling a little foolish at her outburst of emotion. But she couldn't stop her hands from trembling as she carefully undid the package, not knowing what to expect.

'Oh!' she exclaimed, staring in amazement at the beautiful brooch nestling on a cushion of black velvet. 'For me?'

'Yes,' he replied softly.

Spellbound by such a magnificent gift she traced the two golden hearts entwined with a precious stone set in the middle. She knew this was a valuable piece of jewellery because she had often seen Mrs Smith-Allen wear jewellery and she always made a great fuss about its safe-keeping. She gazed up into his eyes.

'But I can't possibly take it. I've never worn anything like this before. Besides, you are saving up to buy your own fishing smack so you cannot afford to buy me such an expensive gift.'

She offered the brooch back to him.

'Hannah, that is why I care so much for you. You're so unselfish, always thinking of others. This brooch was my grandmother's. When I was a small boy in Denmark I stayed with her often and she let me play with her trinket box and I always admired this brooch. Sadly, not long after my parents were drowned, my grandmother died. A friend of my grandmother's recently came over from Denmark and contacted me through the Danish consul, bringing me the brooch my grandmother had bequeathed to me. I could not sell it.

Hannah, you understand? You are the only person I want to wear it.'

'But it is so beautiful,' she enthused, her eyes shining with pleasure.

'Yes, I agree and so are you. Now let me fasten it to the lace collar of your dress.'

She breathed in his nearness, his fresh scent of newly-washed skin and the faint smell of tar and fish that no fisherman could disguise.

'There,' he said, kissing her cheek, making her blush.

Lovingly fingering the brooch she asked, 'What is the precious stone?'

'Topaz. The colour of the stone suits your eyes and your hair.'

Somewhere, a clock struck three and she jumped to her feet.

'Christian, I must go, but you may come back with me for tea.'

It was the least she could offer.

'Yah, I am happy, too.'

He took her arm and placed it through his.

Back at Arden Square, Ruby admired

the brooch and fussed around Christian, cutting him a generous portion of her speciality, a chocolate cake, pleased that her determined efforts to master baking and cooking were beginning to show results. They settled around the table enjoying the warmth of the cosy kitchen, absorbing the aroma of a leg of lamb roasting in the oven for Robert Burnett's evening meal.

But all Hannah wanted to do was feast her eyes on Christian, glad that the misunderstanding between them was resolved. She marvelled that they were spending time together, albeit in Ruby's presence. She moved nearer to him, desperate to feel his body next to hers, to prove she wasn't dreaming.

Christian took her hand in his, saying, 'Time passes too quickly. I must go. I sail on the evening tide.'

Disappointment flooded Hannah's eyes, her voice filled with sadness.

'You are going so soon?'

'I will be back, Hannah, perhaps in three to four weeks. But I will send a message to you so we can spend more time together.'

Tactfully, Ruby found something urgent to do in the scullery as Hannah melted into Christian's strong arms, feeling his tender lips on hers. She responded with an ardour she didn't realise she possessed. She clung tightly to him, willing him never to leave her.

'Hannah, you are mine, I love you. One day we will be together always, I promise you,' he whispered then gently he disentangled himself from her.

She stood on the step, waving him off. She hated the sea, but she knew she could never ask him to give it up. The sea had taken her father, and now her brother, Tom, was fishing. If she and Christian married, which might not be for years because he was saving up to buy his own fishing smack, would she be able to accept the sea?

And then she had Georgie to consider. Like her, he hated the sea. When first they had been admitted into the orphanage, she had vowed that one day they would all live together as a family. Now Tom was fishing and Lily was about to start employment and move into lodgings. Hannah sighed deeply. Life was complicated and perhaps her dream was impossible, but she would endeavour to succeed somehow. The sound of footsteps in the hall behind her jolted her back to the present.

'Are you going to stand on that step for ever?' Ruby exclaimed.

Hannah came in and shut the door. There was work to be done. As she went about her household duties, she replayed in her mind the precious time spent with Christian. That night as she lay in her narrow bed in the attic under the eaves of the roof, she hugged the pillow, wishing it was Christian. Before sleep captured her, she prayed for his safe return.

Meanwhile, downstairs, Robert Burnett rubbed his tired eyes. This new project he was endeavouring to promote was sapping all his mental energy, but not his physical energy. His desire to hold a woman in his arms once again was strong. The problem was he didn't just want any woman. Since the death of his wife, he had not been interested in anyone, until Hannah came into his house.

Now he couldn't stop thinking about her. But would she look at him, a man twenty years older than her? Though from a working-class background, Hannah was educated, able to read and write, with ample common-sense, but what attracted him most were her beauty and the warmth of her caring nature. Earlier, when she'd been serving his evening meal, he found himself staring at her with open adoration. There had been something extra special about her tonight. She positively glowed with radiance and when she smiled at him he felt greatly tempted to take her in his arms.

He rose stiffly from his chair and went over to his cabinet and took out a bottle of brandy. He poured himself a generous measure and gulped it down in one go. Lighting a cigar, he left his study and let himself out the back door that led into the garden. Leaning on the wall, he drew on his cigar and looked lovingly up to the attic window that was Hannah's bedroom.

A week later, on her afternoon off, Hannah went to visit Georgie and Lily at the orphanage. Lily was soon to take up her employment as an apprentice to a dressmaker and move into her new lodgings. She was happy but Georgie sulked.

'You know, Hannah, I don't want to stay here on my own. Why can't I come and live with you?' he pleaded.

Sadly, she took his hands in hers.

'Georgie, when I have a home of my own, then you can. I promise.'

But Georgie couldn't be appeased.

'It's not fair.'

His bottom lip quivered and he kicked at the wooden bench they were sitting on. Hannah couldn't say or do anything to cheer him up. His unhappy face haunted her all the way back to Arden Square.

'I just don't know what to do,' she confided in Ruby.

'Well, yer can't hide him under your bed, that's for sure,' Ruby scoffed.

Hannah busied herself in the kitchen, preparing Robert Burnett's evening meal while Ruby had a couple of hours' free time. Cooking proved therapeutic, helping to take her mind off Georgie's plight. The menu was Ruby's standby, beef casserole. Robert Burnett wouldn't complain, but she thought he might appreciate a change so she decided to make a beef pie.

All though serving Robert's meal, for once her thoughts were not with Christian, but on Georgie. As she cleared away the fish course, she wondered what her brother had eaten for supper. Poor Georgie, all alone in that loveless place. She felt so guilty.

She set the meat dish before Robert, taking off the lid to reveal a steaming beef pie surrounded by an array of tender broad beans and minted potatoes. When she returned to serve the dessert, she found the dishes empty, not a scrap of food to be seen.

'That was excellent, Hannah, so succulent and tasty. But tell me, why do you look so unhappy?'

He raised a quizzical eyebrow, giving her his full attention. Suddenly, as if to unburden herself, she told him about her dilemma over Georgie.

'Poor little chap. You must visit him more often, and perhaps bring him here for a visit.'

'Oh, thank you, sir. He'd like that.'

She felt much happier. Talking to Robert had lightened her heart. For an employer, he was very understanding.

'Hannah, I am a fairly good judge of character and I trust you.'

From the top of his smoking jacket he withdrew a small silver key and laid it on the table between them. She looked at it, puzzled, then at him.

'It is the key to my late wife's bureau. You may use it as your own, perhaps when you attend to the household accounts, or any other matters.'

He smiled at her, rising to his feet.

'I think I will retire to my study now.'

'Yes, sir. I'll bring your port directly.'

When he'd gone, she picked up the key, turning it over in her hand, curious, yet sad, but thrilled to have gained her employer's trust.

The next day, she asked Ruby about the bureau.

'No, I haven't seen inside it, only beeswax it from time to time,' she replied, bustling happily about the kitchen.

'I've to use it for the household accounts, so it'll save me spreading them out on the kitchen table.'

'Aye, you can be a right untidy tyke, Hannah Cullen,' Ruby joked.

She was pleased with Hannah's helping hands. She, Hannah and Jenny worked as a team. The house was no longer in a chaotic state and little Charlotte, bless her, had cut three teeth. Even Mr Burnett seemed happier.

Later on that afternoon, Hannah ventured into the drawing-room and stood before the bureau. Pulling off its dustsheet, she traced her fingers along the well-polished, walnut surface, hesitating. Putting off the moment, her gaze wandered round the room, not used since she'd been there. Perhaps the presence of the late Mrs Burnett still lingered, beneath the mounds of dustsheets. She shivered. The key burned in the palm of her hand. She sighed; she had nothing to fear.

The key turned quite easily in the lock. The lid came down to form a writing desk inlaid with brown leather edged with a gold-leaf design. She peered at the shaped interior fittings. There were six uncluttered tiny drawers, three at either side of the centre cupboard. The cupboard was locked and as far as she was concerned it could stay locked. She had no need of it, unless Robert Burnett dictated otherwise.

Drawing up one of the high-backed

chairs, she made herself comfortable. Replenishing the inkwell, she spread out the tradesmen's bills and receipts on the desk, keeping them in date order, along with the butcher's weight tickets that she'd insisted on receiving to check against the weight of the meat. When she'd studied the previous housekeeper's accounts, she found them in quite a muddle with a number of inaccurate entries.

Hannah endeavoured to be more careful by double-checking each entry she made. Proudly she opened her housekeeping book, supplied by Robert, smoothing back the pages adorned by her neat copperplate writing that her mother had taught her. She let her gaze linger on Robert's scrawling signature after each weekly inspection.

After a few weeks, usually when the house was quiet on a Sunday afternoon, with Jenny and Charlotte out for a breath of fresh air, and Ruby snoozing in the warmth of the kitchen, Robert

Burnett took tea with her in the drawing-room. He had insisted on her using the whole room, not just the bureau.

'Otherwise, Hannah, it will become a musty museum. I want Charlotte to grow up in a happy atmosphere.'

She smiled at him.

'I have to agree, sir.'

★　★　★

The nights grew longer and the days became shorter, and soon the Christmas season would be upon them. Hannah waited for news of Christian's homecoming, but it never came. She kept her eye on the newspaper seller's placard for any fishing smacks missing, but none was.

'His talk must come cheap,' she remarked bitterly to Ruby one day as they worked in the kitchen preparing for Christmas.

'Aye, well, he might have got himself wed to the lass you saw him kissing.

45

And if he has, she isn't gonna let him call on you,' Ruby commented vigorously, stirring the plum pudding.

Hannah, setting the basins on the table in readiness for the puddings, replied passionately, 'That can't be true. Christian loves me and we are to marry one day.'

Hannah stared into space. Had she misread Christian's intentions? Was it her own fault by saying that she hated the sea when he obviously loved it? But he had given her his grandmother's precious brooch. Surely that was a declaration of love. She would have gone down to the Humber Dock and asked Jonas if he had news of the Saint Beaut, but she was so busy with the preparations for the festive season. Her mind was in a turmoil with mixed emotions, sending her head into a spin. She would have loved to escape to her room and lie down for a while and rest, but there was work to be done.

When serving dinner that evening,

Robert Burnett noticed Hannah's subdued preoccupation. Believing it was Georgie on her mind, he decided the time was right to tell her of his little plan.

'Hannah, what are the orphanage's plans for Christmas Day?'

For a second she stared blankly at him, then remembering her position, quickly replied.

'I believe, sir, the same as any other day, except they go to church like on a Sunday.'

'In that case, I would like to extend a cordial invitation for Georgie to spend the day with us. I shall write accordingly to the master at the orphanage. In the meantime, you may pass on the news to your brother.'

'Oh, sir, that's wonderful, truly. Georgie will be pleased and so am I.'

She felt her spirits lifting. Robert was also pleased. He couldn't bear to see her unhappy. Her presence in his house was becoming vital to his daily living. Charlotte brought laughter into his life.

She was depending upon him, holding out her arms for him to swing her high, and he was becoming dependent upon Hannah. He thought about her every day, knowing each evening when he returned home from business, she would be waiting to greet him. She radiated a strength that reached his heart, a feeling he'd never experienced before.

A few days later, Hannah had a surprise visit from Tom and a girl of his own age, sixteen.

'We're walking out,' Tom said proudly, puffing out his chest. 'Gladys lives with her mother who has a corner shop next to my lodgings.'

They sat in the cosy kitchen around the table, drinking tea and eating Ruby's chocolate cake.

'That's nice, Tom. I'm pleased for you. More cake?'

Then, leaning back in her chair, she thought how quickly Tom had grown up. He was a young man now. A tinge of sadness pulled at her heart, knowing the chance of them all sharing a home together was becoming more remote.

'Seen our Lily, Tom?' Hannah asked, keeping the conversation going.

'Snatched a few words with her, but she was on her way out with that mate of hers.'

'I'm going to pop over and see her before Christmastime. Have you seen Christian?' she added.

Tom fiddled with a loose button on his jacket. Avoiding Hannah's eyes he mumbled.

'Saw him a couple of days ago. He was just about to sail.'

Hannah sat up straight.

'You saw Christian? But he promised to come and see me! Are you sure he was sailing?'

'Aye.'

Tom scrambled to his feet, pulling Gladys up with him.

'We have to go now. Thanks for tea.'

Outside, Gladys poked Tom in the ribs.

'I thought you had a note to give

Hannah from Christian.'

'I tore it up. I don't want my sister to marry that foreigner.'

Inside, Hannah remained at the kitchen table. She covered her face with her hands and let herself sink into total dejection. How could Christian treat her this way? She had believed in him and he had betrayed her. He'd broken his promise to visit her. His words had come so cheap.

Then an idea sprang into her confused mind. What if she went round to his lodgings and confronted the landlady's daughter and demanded the truth? Was she walking out with Christian? Then, appalled at her self-pity and her lack of pride, Hannah raised her head high and pushed back her chair. Her eyes bright and fiery, she shouted out angrily.

'Damn you, Christian Hansen,' she yelled, frightening a startled Ruby who was just entering the kitchen.

★　★　★

Georgie couldn't contain his excitement. He was thrilled to be spending a whole day away from the orphanage. On Christmas Day, he arrived at Arden Square at ten in the morning attired in smart navy trousers and matching jersey, and highly-polished boots.

On being introduced to Robert Burnett, Georgie bowed and said, 'Good morning, sir. Very good of you to invite me into your home.'

Hannah bubbled with pride. She suspected he'd been rehearsing that little speech for some time, and she had to admit that the discipline of the orphanage had helped to turn him into a well-mannered boy.

Robert beamed, impressed.

'Welcome to my home.'

The day was a glorious success. It reminded Hannah of her childhood Christmases, though on a grander scale, but with the same warmth and good humour. Happy laughter filled each room as a tottering Charlotte was

51

chasing a blindfolded Georgie.

There were gasps as everyone sat down at the dining table, which Hannah had decorated with springs of holly and evergreens gathered at first light from the garden. Robert Burnett supplied a well-stocked table, with glazed duck, roast beef, an array of vegetables and sauces, plaice decorated with lemon and parsley, desserts of jellies, snow cake, almond spice biscuits and a rich fruit pudding, flowing with the aroma of French brandy white sauce.

Under the great fir tree decorated with lit candles were parcels wrapped in thin blue tissue paper. There was a small gift for everyone. Hannah had often worked late into the night making mufflers for Charlotte, Jenny and Ruby, sweets for Georgie, and for Robert she rescued one of his frayed waistcoats, carefully repaired it, then embroidered on the front two quills in bold red, which represented the sign above his shop premises.

He held it high, inspecting her delicate work.

'Hannah, this is truly a marvellous gift, so personal. I shall wear it every Sunday when we take tea.'

She felt herself blush as Ruby gave her a funny look.

Later, Hannah walked with Georgie back to the orphanage. Robert wanted to send for a cab but Hannah declined. It was such a lovely evening and after the excitement of the day and eating so much rich food, she welcomed the walk. The sky, velvety blue, was aglow with an abundance of stars shining bright on the cold, night air. She clasped Georgie's hand and felt the warmth of his tired body as he leaned into hers.

'I like your house, Hannah,' he murmured. 'Why can't I come and live with you?'

She squeezed his hand, her heart aching as she answered.

'Oh, Georgie, love. If only you could. It would make me so happy. But you can come and visit often. Mr Burnett is so kind.'

Soon the household reverted to its normal routine after Christmas and one morning, a few days later, Jenny slipped on an icy patch in the yard, twisting her ankle.

'I felt such a fool,' she remarked to Hannah. 'The butcher boy was just making his delivery, but he was ever so kind and helped me up.'

Hannah nodded sympathetically, knowing that Jenny was sweet on the boy. Gently she bathed the swollen ankle.

'You'll have to rest it for awhile,' she said, soaking a clean strip of sheeting in a lotion of witch-hazel. 'I'll strap this round your ankle and it will help to soothe the bruising and give you support. Now, lie back on the chair while I ease the footstool under your feet. There, is that comfortable?'

'Yes, thank you,' Jenny replied. 'What will Mr Burnett say?'

'I'm sure he'll understand. Besides, I

can look after Charlotte for a day or two, and now the washerwoman's daughter comes every morning to light the fires, wash the front step and polish the brass, it gives me time to do other things. I love Charlotte and want to spend more time with her.'

'But tomorrow, I'm supposed to be going to chapel with the master and Charlotte,' she said, wincing as a spasm of pain shot through her ankle.

Downstairs in the kitchen, Hannah put the problem to Ruby.

'Oh, Hannah, chapel isn't my line. I'd rather stay in and work.'

'I'll go then,' Hannah decided.

She explained the position to Robert.

'That's quite all right, Hannah. I look forward to you accompanying Charlotte and me to chapel.'

Sunday morning came and Hannah dressed with care in her best grey dress for her first outing with her employer. Sprinkling rose water on to her fine linen handkerchief, a Christmas gift from Robert, she inhaled the delicate perfume. About her shoulders she slipped a mantle of warm, soft wool and fixing her black hat trimmed with artificial flowers on to her neatly arranged hair, she surveyed her appearance critically in the mirror above her dressing table.

Her eyes strayed to her trinket box that had been her dear mother's. Inside was the brooch Christian had given her. It would add the final touch to her ensemble, but would it be right? Now, if she was betrothed to Christian . . . She sighed deeply. Stop it, Hannah Cullen, and put all thoughts of that particular young man out of her head. She pulled a face at herself. Leaving her room, she wondered if Robert Burnett would find her appearance pleasing.

As she was making her way to the nursery to collect Charlotte, Ruby came puffing up the stairs.

'Come quickly. You've got a visitor.'

'Who?'

'You'll see.'

Hannah fully expected to see Lily waiting in the kitchen.

'Hannah,' the visitor said as he held out his arms.

She stood framed in the doorway.

'Christian!'

Her hands instinctively came up to her face, together, as if in prayer. He was the last person she expected to see.

'You are pleased to see me, yah?'

His arms fell to his side, and her face was grim as she stepped into the kitchen.

'What are you doing here?' she snapped.

The smile vanished from Christian's face.

'Hannah! What are you saying?'

'Why have you come here? You think that you can come into my life then abandon me then casually drop in and expect me to welcome you with open arms? I can tell you, Christian Hansen, it does not work!'

Her eyes blazed and her body shook

with fury as she faced him. He put out his hand to steady her and she knocked it away.

'Hannah, Hannah! Why are you so upset?'

He couldn't understand her, when all he wanted to do was to take her in his arms and hold her close. He'd missed her so much.

'You promised me the next time you were home you would come and see me, but you didn't. Don't deny it because our Tom saw you.'

'I was only in port for twelve hours then we had to put to sea again. I wrote you a note and asked Tom to deliver it to you, explaining.'

'What note?' she replied heatedly.

'Didn't you see Tom?'

'Yes, but he didn't give me a note.'

Ruby chose that moment to enter the kitchen, saying to Hannah, 'Time's getting on.'

Christian, anxious for this misunderstanding to be cleared up and aware of Ruby's watchful eye, said, 'Hannah, you are dressed for walking. Shall we go out?'

Thinking how beautiful she looked with her face flushed to a delicate pink, dressed so attractively, his arms ached to hold her. He desired her so much, and he had so much to tell her.

'I'm sorry, Christian, but I'm going to chapel with my employer.'

Not to be deterred he said, 'Later, this afternoon we can meet, no?'

Hannah thought of her usual Sunday afternoon meeting with Robert Burnett. Perhaps if Jenny had not been indisposed?

'It's not possible today. Maybe tomorrow afternoon, I'll try and snatch an hour off.'

Christian's face clouded with a dark sadness.

'Too late. I sail on the morning tide.'

'Oh. Then next time you're home, send me word beforehand, maybe with your landlady's daughter,' she added waspishly, hating herself.

He caught her hand roughly in his.

'Walk with me across the square.'

Still holding hands, she followed him from the house, stopping near to the Prince Street corner. He pulled her close, and she felt his powerful muscles strain as he fought to control his emotions.

'Hannah, do not let us become enemies,' he said sadly.

'It is you who is not truthful.'

Tears filled her eyes.

'Please, Hannah, let us remain friends.'

She nodded, not trusting herself to speak. Then his lips softly brushed her cheek, but she held back from him. He sighed deeply.

'I will not keep you from your work. Goodbye for now, Hannah.'

She watched him go, her heart full of misgivings. Slowly, head down, she retraced her steps back to the house.

From his bedroom window, Robert Burnett had witnessed the scene between Hannah and Christian, and it disturbed him, arousing in him jealous thoughts. Hannah shone with warmth and beauty, lighting up his life. He had not considered the possibility of someone else thinking the same. But it was evident. He'd seen the way that the young, handsome fisherman courted Hannah with just a touch and a look.

Robert turned from the window. The muscles in his eyes flexed, the beat of his heart quickened. He was not going to let her go. He strode purposefully from the room and into the nursery.

'My little angel, come here.'

He swept Charlotte up into his arms.

'You are going to have a new mama!'

3

January was a cold, bleak month. Winds up to gale force swept the seas and the fishing community of Kingston-upon-Hull clustered around the Humber Dock was devastated when three smacks, on three consecutive days, ran aground, going down with all hands lost.

Hannah went out each day to check the newspaper seller's placard, and then she would slip into Betchy Street Chapel and pray for the safe return of Tom and Christian. On the third day she read the placard with horror. The Saint Beaut had gone down with all hands.

'Christian, oh, Christian,' she wailed.

Unable to hide her grief, not caring who saw or heard her, she ran through the streets to the chapel. Collapsing on a pew, she sobbed, her heart breaking.

Then remorse and guilt began to grip her as she remembered her last meeting with Christian, when she had sent him away in such an uncaring way. Now she would never have the chance to tell him how much she loved him.

Her body ached with stiffness and cold but she remained in her cramped position for what seemed hours until she felt a gentle hand touch her shoulder. Raising her head she looked up into the concerned face of the Reverend Rendell. She had met him on occasions when she attended chapel with Robert Burnett.

'My child, you are grieving. The fishing smacks?'

'The Saint Beaut,' she whispered painfully.

'And the name of your loved one?'

'Christian Hansen,' she said with a proud tilt of her head.

'The young Danish man. A good man.'

He kneeled down beside her and

clasped her hands warmly in his for a few seconds.

'Shall we pray together for your loved one and for all the loved ones lost in these terrible tragedies?'

Through hot, seething tears, Hannah prayed for Christian that he might find eternal rest. Then after moments of quiet reflection, the clergyman rose to his feet, assisting Hannah to her feet.

'I must go. The bereaved, there are so many I must see and comfort. Go home and remember you are always welcome in God's house. Bless you.'

In a trance, Hannah went outside, slowly making her way back to Arden Square. On entering the house she was met by a fractious Ruby.

'You took your time. Charlotte keeps being sick and is crying for you.'

Without a word, Hannah hurried up the staircase to the nursery. Gathering the tearful Charlotte up in her arms, she held her close, drawing solace from the warmth of the child's body.

Charlotte, suffering a tummy upset,

clung to Hannah and for a while Hannah forgot her grief. She gave Jenny the evening off, taking care of the child herself, playing with her, bathing her and giving her supper. Then they sat quietly in front of the nursery fire listening to Robert read a bedtime story. In this moment of solitude she reflected on the sadness of Christian's death, remembering the happy times they had shared together, and in a fitting tribute to his memory she decided to wear his grandmother's brooch as a token of their love. As she listened to Robert's animated voice and Charlotte's laughter, a quiet peace descended on her, but the image of Christian in a watery grave would be with her for ever.

In the days after the news of Christian's death, Hannah kept herself very busy. Humbled by the brave women who had lost their husbands in the fishing tragedy, she helped out at Reverend Rendell's soup kitchen. Christian, her first love, the man she should have given more care to, had gone, but these women had lost more. They had lost their breadwinners and they had children to support.

Each morning, she rose early and went along to the chapel, helping to prepare the daily soup for the hungry and the bereaved. She was able to draw a small comfort for her efforts and share in the camaraderie that sprang up between the fishermen's widows.

One crisp, bright morning she returned from the chapel to find a formal note delivered to her from the orphanage. It requested her presence as soon as possible. Hannah didn't delay, fearful that something had happened to Georgie. Leaving Ruby in charge of the household she made haste. On arriving at the orphanage she was kept waiting in the airless ante-room for what seemed for ever before a young girl appeared.

'Matron will see you now, miss,' she said.

In comparison to the ante-room,

matron's room was light and bright with a large window overlooking the courtyard.

'Please, be seated, Miss Cullen,' Matron said, indicating a wooden chair.

Matron sat down on a comfortable, well-upholstered chair behind a huge desk, her manner brisk.

'Georgie was eleven last week,' she began, 'and arrangements have been made for him to take a trip on one of Mr Smith-Allen's fishing smacks.'

Hannah's blood turned ice-cold, then just as quick it boiled. She jumped to her feet.

'No! Our Georgie is not going to sea.'

The startled woman replied, 'The arrangements have been made and you have no say in the matter, Miss Cullen.'

'That's where you're wrong.'

Words just tumbled from her mouth.

'I've made arrangements of my own. My employer, Mr Burnett, has given permission for Georgie to lodge with me, and he has promised him employment.'

The expression on the matron's face was one of disbelief. Hannah hurried to the door.

'I'll be back tomorrow for Georgie. Please have his belongings ready. Good day.'

Jerking open the door, she fled from the orphanage before Matron could ask her any questions. Only when she was safely inside the kitchen at Arden Square did she stop to draw breath.

'Goodness!' Ruby exclaimed, when Hannah finished telling her what she'd done. 'What are you gonna do? Hide young Georgie away from the master?'

'No, I can't do that. I'll have to tell him and just hope that he isn't in a strange mood.'

That evening, Hannah was puzzled. It wasn't like Robert Burnett to be as quiet as he was. Hannah wondered if he might be having problems at his printing works. He had mentioned to her some weeks ago that he was negotiating a special order. Serving dinner, Hannah returned his untouched dishes to the sideboard. This wasn't the best of times to approach him, but she had no choice.

'Please, sir,' she began, facing him.

He looked up into her anxious face. 'Yes, what is it?'

He didn't mean his voice to sound so abrupt. He watched the soft skin of her cheeks flush to a delicate pink.

'Please, sir, may I have a word with you? It's very important.'

His throat tightened. He rose from the table.

'I will take my port in the study. You may join me there in ten minutes.'

In his room, Robert slumped in his armchair, staring into the fire. His head ached. He now believed he'd finally clinched the deal to print the invitation cards for the forthcoming royal visit. Tomorrow he would know for certain, then he was going to speak to Hannah about taking Georgie on as an apprentice. But was it too late? Was she about to tell him she was leaving for new employment or going off to marry that fisherman?

He didn't know of Christian's death. He only knew that he couldn't face the prospect of not seeing Hannah each day, a daunting thought. Her lively presence in the house gave him strength to face each new morning.

There came a polite tap at the door and Hannah entered, placing the tray on the small table next to his chair. He sat up straight, facing her. Better to get it over and done with, he remonstrated with himself.

'Now, what is so important that it cannot wait?' he asked.

Her face muscles twitched as she forced a smile.

'It's good of you to see me, sir.'

In spite of her smile he noticed her lovely eyes held a nervous look. He felt an overwhelming desire to take her into his arms and hold her closely in his arms. He closed his eyes. Why was he tormenting himself?

'Are you all right, sir?' she asked.

Her hand touched his arm, its

warmth melting through the material of his jacket. He opened his eyes and the room seemed to revolve as his body swayed forward. Her touch on his arm tightened to a strong grip and she leaned across him, the full softness of her body pushing against his as she eased him back in his chair. He breathed in her perfume of a summer rose. He lay back in his chair, his eyes glazed, staring at her blurred outline as she hovered above him.

'Have a drink of your port, sir,' she said, holding the glass to his lips.

The port ran down his throat like bitter fire, seeping through his body and returning life to his limbs. He focused his eyes on Hannah's anxious face.

'I'm sorry. It's just that I can't bear the thought of you leaving.'

'Leaving? But I don't understand, sir. I'm not leaving.'

He looked at her not sure if he'd heard her correctly.

'You're not?'

71

'No, sir. It is Georgie I wish to speak to you about.'

'Georgie?'

'I have a problem, sir.'

He sighed with relief.

'Sit down, Hannah, and tell me.'

When she'd finished, he spoke gently.

'We have both been foolish, but one thing I know for certain. You are very dear to me, Hannah.'

She blushed, lowering her lashes. Robert brimmed with a new invigoration of hope, speaking confidently now.

'Georgie is a bright lad, well mannered. I believe he has the right attitude for learning the trade and that he will make a good apprentice. I did intend to speak to you tomorrow about taking him on, when I will know for certain my current financial circumstances, but that's irrelevant now. I will write a letter for the orphanage, setting out my responsibility for Georgie.'

Slowly Hannah rose to her feet, overcome with emotion.

'You mean Georgie . . . he can come here?'

'Yes.'

He watched the happiness spread across her face. So young and beautiful, would she consider a man twenty years her senior? He stood up and reached out to take hold of her hands. She looked at him, so trusting.

'Hannah, I have a very important question to ask you.'

Her honey-coloured eyes, so young and innocent, watched his lips, causing his body to heat up rapidly.

'Will you do me the honour of becoming my wife?'

Her face paled. Her eyes searched his.

Oh, no, he thought, I've rushed it.

'Sir, I — '

He held up his hand to silence her.

'Hannah, no matter what your decision is Georgie still comes. I just want you to consider my proposal.'

Hannah didn't sleep that night. Her mind was tormented with images of

Christian kissing her passionately and holding her so tight that their bodies melted together. She knew Robert Burnett was a kind, generous man and she respected him, but she didn't love him, and she yearned to love and be loved. She buried her face in the pillow, crying for her lost love.

Next morning as she served breakfast to Robert she tried to act as normal as possible, but she couldn't. She felt awkward and her words seemed stilted. Robert was very formal.

When he gave her the letter to take to the orphanage regarding Georgie's release, she could only say, 'Thank you, sir.'

Ruby, detecting an atmosphere, asked, 'You and master had a row?'

Not wanting to tell her friend the whole truth she replied, 'No, of course not. It's to do with Georgie.'

'Is he letting Georgie come then?'

'Yes.'

Hannah hurried from the dining-room, frightened of any more questions. If

Ruby persisted, she would weaken and tell her of Robert's proposal of marriage, and Ruby, though her friend, was a profound gossip and would tell the trades' people who called at the house. No, she had to think this through on her own.

When Jenny took Charlotte out for her afternoon airing, Hannah slipped away to the chapel. Here she found solitude. Wrestling with her conscience, she tried to talk in her mind to Christian about Robert's proposal, but Christian was not with her in spirit. So much anguish filled her head and body that she didn't hear the Reverend Rendell approaching.

'Hannah, my dear, are you all right?'

Over the past few weeks he had come to know Hannah and respected her determination in helping others less fortunate than herself. She brushed away a fallen tear, her heart weighed down. She met the steady gaze of this kindly man, unleashing her jumbled thoughts on him.

He sat beside her in the pew and listened until all her words were spent then he spoke quietly.

'My dear, Christian wouldn't want you to be unhappy. Even though your parting was tinged with sadness, I feel sure he understands and there is no need for guilt. Robert Burnett is an admirable man and he will take care of you and in return you will make him happy. I'm certain you will, my dear.'

He rose from the pew.

'Think about what I have said and come back if you need to talk further.'

'Thank you. I feel better already for talking to you.'

On her way home, she made a detour home via Humber Dock. Standing on the quayside, she looked across the wide expanse of the Humber. Its waters were so calm it was difficult for her to imagine it at its most perilous, flowing out to the great North Sea whose treachery knew no bounds.

'Goodbye, Christian,' she whispered

sadly. 'I'll never forget you.'

That evening, she made Robert Burnett a very happy man. She promised herself that she would be a good and dutiful wife to him.

4

Robert Burnett was ecstatic, his enthusiasm transmitting to every member of his household and his small workforce.

'I shall place a notice of our marriage in the Hull News. Then I shall speak to the Reverend Rendell. As it is my second marriage, I wish it to be a quiet affair, but of the very best. Don't you agree, Hannah?'

'Yes, Robert.'

They were sitting on high-backed chairs in the drawing-room, her room as she now thought of it. Her bureau had pride of place in front of the long window overlooking the square. This would become her sitting-room, her private place to sit and dream, and of course for her and Robert to have tea together as they usually did on a Sunday afternoon. For the first time, since Christian's reported death, she breathed a sigh of contentment.

'Hannah, are you listening?'

'Sorry, Robert.'

She kept her eyes fixed on his beaming face.

'I like the Reverend Rendell. He is so kind,' she said.

'And you are a worthy person, helping him run his soup kitchen.'

She blushed.

'I didn't realise you knew about that.'

'I know everything about you, Hannah Cullen.'

He rose from his chair and, coming over to her, he took her hand in his, kissing it tenderly.

'I want us to be married as soon as possible. March, I think, would be admirable. Do you agree, Hannah?'

'Yes, Robert,' she murmured, suddenly feeling panic-stricken.

What would Robert expect of her as a wife? She had so little time to get used to the idea.

'First I must write to Mr Smith-Allen, a man of importance and at one time responsible for your welfare, and seek his permission.'

Hannah had completely forgotten about Edward Smith-Allen. Robert continued talking in the same enthusiastic manner.

'Now, I've arranged for Georgie to lodge at the home of one of my workers. Mr Pringles and his wife are a pleasant, caring couple who have two small boys. Then when we are married, Georgie can have your old room.'

At the mention of her brother, Hannah's face lit up.

'A room of his own! He'll love that.'

So, she thought, Robert was a man of his word, not that she had ever doubted him. Georgie was leaving the orphanage later today and she was to take him to Robert's place of business in Market Place for a formal introduction. The business consisted of a shop selling books and stationery, and in the workshop at the back of the shop, Robert had set up a small printing press which he was in the throes of developing. It was here that Georgie was to start his apprenticeship.

★ ★ ★

'Fancy you been gone on Mr Burnett,' Ruby marvelled to Hannah as she thumped the dough she was preparing. 'I don't know how yer could have kept it so quiet.'

Hannah lowered her head, busying herself putting away some clean pinafores in the kitchen drawer.

'And a wedding in March! By heck, that's a first for me, a wedding breakfast. Oh, Hannah, I don't think I can do it. Cook for all those posh people.'

At the sound of her friend's frantic voice, Hannah spun round.

'Of course you can, Ruby. Just think of all the cooking you did at Christmas and that didn't worry you. We can hire extra help.'

Ruby stared at Hannah.

'Do you mean it?'

81

'Yes. You can do it.'

'Well, if you say so.'

'And there aren't any posh people coming, just some of Robert's business acquaintances and their wives, and his aunt.'

Hannah had met Robert's aunt only once. She was a tall, thin woman, widowed, with no children, who lived quietly on the northern fringe of the city, near to Pearson Park. A woman prone to being indisposed, so Hannah had heard.

Later that day, in the afternoon, Hannah glanced out of the drawing-room window at the bright February sky. She fancied a walk but it was out of the question as she was so busy. She turned from the window and went back to sewing her wedding trousseau. She hummed a little tune, surprised how happy and contented she felt.

Robert had wanted her to go to a dressmaker's, but she had insisted on making her own garments for her wedding. She purchased materials, thread and trimmings from the local general drapers where Robert had opened an account for her. This was a new experience for her and although Robert's allowance was generous, she would not spend a farthing more than necessary.

Suddenly the door opened and Jenny entered the room carrying a tray laden with a jug of fresh, tangy lemonade and a plate of sweet, almond biscuits.

'Hanni.'

The cherub figure of Charlotte hidden behind Jenny's skirt emerged and teetered on unsteady legs towards Hannah.

'My angel.'

Hannah put down her needle and scooped Charlotte up in her arms.

'You come to share lemonade and biscuits with me?'

Jenny put the tray on a low table near to the fireplace and Hannah carried Charlotte over.

'She's been fretting for you and won't have her afternoon nap till she's seen you,' Jenny said slightly peeved. 'And I've got her clothes to iron. Washerwoman said they're too fiddly for her to do.'

Hannah sat on the sofa, bouncing a laughing Charlotte on her knee.

'Leave her with me and you go and do your ironing.'

'Are you sure?' Jenny asked rather timidly.

'Yes. I want to spend more time with this little angel and maybe we will have a little walk in the garden.'

Jenny disappeared fast, just in case Hannah changed her mind.

The day of Robert's and Hannah's wedding finally dawned, a crisp March morning with a dazzling blue sky. Hannah threw a shawl over her nightgown and went downstairs, slipping out the back door leading into the garden. Here, as she walked on the dewy path, she relished the quiet solitude, drawing strength for the day ahead.

She had had private thoughts,

remembering Christian. How different she would be feeling if she were marrying him. Shivering, she went back into the house, seeking the warmth of the kitchen where Ruby had just made a pot of tea. Snatching a hot drink, she refused Ruby's offer of food.

'Saving yourself for the wedding breakfast?' Ruby asked.

'Of course,' Hannah said lightly.

She hurried from the kitchen, her stomach churning. Upstairs on the landing she passed Robert's room. Tonight it would be their room. She didn't want to think about tonight though she was pleased about the bedroom. Gone were the heavy drapes and dark wallpaper, the choice of his first wife. Hannah had concentrated on making the room light with the help of the paperhangers and painters Robert engaged. They transformed the room with warm shades of primrose and a subtle shade of blue, and she herself made the drapes, picking up a richness of both colours.

Robert's contribution was a new bed with a shining, elaborate mahogany headboard and two matching chairs. Her heart sank at the thought of the marriage bed. Hannah sighed deeply, wishing her beloved mother were alive to advise her on what was expected of her.

Welcoming shrieks of laughter floated from the nursery and Hannah stopped to peer through the open door. Charlotte was doing a jig, looking so pretty dressed in an embroidered, muslin dress with twin flounces supported by layers of petticoats. The apricot-coloured ribbons in her fair wispy curls spun out as she twirled.

On seeing Hannah in the doorway, Charlotte rushed to her, flinging herself into Hannah's arms.

'Wedding, Hanni,' she cooed.

Hugging the child, taking care not to crush her dress, Hannah then took hold of her hand and drew her back into the room.

'You look so beautiful, my angel. Your

papa will be so proud of you. Now you must sit quietly as we don't want you falling asleep in chapel.'

'We'll sit and play with the building blocks,' Jenny said who looked very smart in her full-skirted new dress of dove grey.

Up in her attic room, soon to be Georgie's, Hannah laid out her new under garments — petticoats, chemise, stockings and the corset, a necessary under-garment to enhance the shape of the figure, so the knowledgeable assistant at Marris & Willow had informed her.

She sat down at her little dressing-table tucked in a corner and sprinkled rosewater on to a clean square of linen. Gently patting her face in tiny circular movements, she relieved her tension, it was so soothing and refreshing.

The night before, Robert had presented her with an intriguing packet tied up with a pretty floppy bow of ribbon with instructions not to open it until today. She eased the bow off the package and carefully she undid the white tissue paper. She gazed in wonderment at the gleaming, silver-backed hairbrush.

Tracing her fingers over the exquisite design of raised flowers entwined with a garland of leaves trailing down the handle, she stopped at the initials HB. She gave a gasp, realising that those initials would soon be hers.

Her gift to Robert was modest in comparison. It was an old pewter inkwell she had bought from a travelling peddler, reputed to be from a sale at a country house. She'd given her gift to Robert last night and he had been enraptured with it.

'A capstan-shaped inkwell, probably seventeenth century,' he had exclaimed, examining the gift.

Leisurely she now brushed her long chestnut hair, letting the brush glide down her curls that shone like a skein of silk. She drifted dreamily on a golden cloud, to think that she Hannah Cullen, once of the orphanage, was to marry the respected businessman, Robert Burnett. Suddenly loud voices and a loud rap on the door broke into her reverie. Lily entered, smelling strongly of sweet violets, and Georgie followed.

'Georgie Cullen,' Lily rebuked, 'it isn't fitting for a lad to see the bride before she dresses. Get off with you.'

'Go on you, Lily. Let me give Hannah a quick hug before she gets poshed up.'

Hannah hugged Georgie close, looking into his broad face. He was now taller than she was and because of the good food he was receiving at his lodgings he was filling out. Pride surged through her. Robert had reported that Georgie was working well under supervision in the printing shop.

'Now be off with you,' she chided, gently pushing him away.

'Come on,' Lily said impatiently. 'You don't want to be late for your own wedding.'

After much chattering and laughing, the bride was finally dressed, except for her hat.

'Do you think it's about right?' Hannah asked anxiously.

She stared at her reflection in the mirror, adjusting the veil over the brim. Lily peered over her shoulder.

'You forgot the flower.'

She fixed the pink artificial rose to the hat.

'You look so pretty.'

Hannah stared at herself. The soft pink of her clear skin matched the velvet of the rose. Standing up, she lifted the skirt of her cream silk dress, trimmed with a single flounce of pink tulle edged with lace caught up at the front with a pink bow, and she twirled with feverish excitement.

'Be careful, I don't think those shoes will last,' Lily remarked with a touch of envy.

Hannah glanced at her black gros-grain shoes with cream cords and chenille pompoms. She could offer no excuse for her wanton extravagance.

'Try these for size,' Lily said thrusting a pair of satin and lace gloves at Hannah.

Easing them on, she whispered, her eyes sparkling, 'They are beautiful.'

She kissed Lily, something she hadn't ever done.

'Hannah, the carriage's here,' Georgie called up.

He had the honour of escorting her to Betchy Street Chapel in place of Tom who was away at sea. She descended the stairs looking every inch a bride. Ruby came bustling from her kitchen to wish Hannah good luck.

'I wish you were coming to the chapel,' Hannah said, a catch in her voice.

'I'll be here when you get back. I'll do yer proud, Hannah Cullen.'

Hannah turned away quickly, her thoughts suddenly full of Christian Hansen. She felt weak and slipped her arm through Georgie's for support. He looked quite the gentleman in coat and trousers made for him by Robert's tailor.

Outside on the step, she breathed in the invigorating air, recovering her strength. After all, she had made a vow to herself to make Robert a good wife and now that vow was going to be made before God. Both Hannah and Georgie gasped in amazement as they stared at the fine carriage bearing the Smith-Allen crest. Edward Smith-Allen had sent his carriage for Hannah's use on her wedding day. It was polished to perfection and attended by two grooms wearing military-styled uniforms of dark green. Georgie whistled.

'If our mam could see us now,' he exclaimed excitedly.

Spring sunlight shone on Hannah as she was helped into the carriage. She sank back into the luxury of the padded velvet upholstery that cushioned her body against the jolting as they rode over the cobbled road.

Hannah alighted from the carriage in a daze, glad of Georgie's supporting arm as they entered the chapel. Inside the chapel, bathed in the celestial lights of many candles, a shiver suddenly ran through her body and panic gripped her. Christian, Christian, she cried silently.

Georgie squeezed her arm affectionately and she held her head high. The organist struck a cord and slowly they moved down the aisle to the haunting music of Mendelssohn.

Much later, as the day came to an end, and all the guests had gone, Charlotte was tucked up in bed, Jenny was asleep, and Robert had escaped to his study to drink port. Hannah went to find Ruby and Georgie in the kitchen. She stood unseen in the open doorway. Ruby was dozing in front of the fire, while Georgie was sitting at the table engrossed in one of Robert's books, munching from a big plate of leftover titbits and drinking ale from a great tankard.

To see Georgie so happy and contented filled her heart with joy.

She'd achieved a home for him. Slowly she retreated and made her way upstairs to Robert's room, now her room as well. A fire burned brightly in the grate and the soft glow of a lamp circled the walls. Crossing over to the window she pulled aside the curtains to peer out on the silent square below and glanced above at the galaxy of stars twinkling down on her. She turned away. There was nothing left but to begin her evening toiletry.

After undressing and slipping on a fine cotton nightgown trimmed with lace, she sat at the walnut dressing-table. She glanced around the magnificent room with awe. Never in her whole life had she slept in a room so grand.

Suddenly the bedroom door opened and Robert entered. Observing him through the mirror, she noticed his face was drawn and tired-looking. Her heart raced hopefully. Maybe tonight he would just want to sleep. She forced a cheery smile. Then, as if by magic, his whole face illuminated. He came up behind her, placing his hands tenderly on the cream of her neck and kissed her cheek. She caught a whiff of tobacco and the warm scent of his maleness. She closed her eyes tightly.

In the mirror, Robert saw her frightened face. He must be very gentle with his lovely, innocent bride.

5

Hannah, Hannah where are you?' Robert called out like an excited boy as he entered the house one evening a few weeks later.

Jenny came into the hall carrying Charlotte's supper tray set with a mug of warm milk and sweet biscuits.

'Mrs Burnett's in the nursery, sir.'

Robert flung his hat and coat on to the hallstand and raced up the stairs with the vigour of a man half his age, much to the amazement of Jenny. She stood transfixed staring up at him.

Hannah was kneeling beside an oblong-shaped tin bowl, bathing Charlotte. She looked up as he dashed into the room, his face radiant, his hand clutching an envelope.

'It's incredible. I knew the authorities were pleased with the royal invitations I printed because they paid me handsomely, but this reward is beyond my dreams.'

Hannah reached for the towel warming by the fire and, lifting Charlotte from her bath, she wrapped the towel around her sweet-scented body and began gently patting her dry. As she did so, she glanced up again waiting for him to continue speaking, but he didn't.

'Robert?'

At that moment, Jenny entered the room and took charge of the little girl and Hannah ushered Robert from the room into their bedroom. She motioned to him by her side on the small sofa by the fireplace.

'Now, Robert, tell me your good news.'

His hands trembled as he withdrew from the envelope a beautifully-designed card, cream with gold-embossed lettering of the highest quality. He passed it to Hannah. She looked at it.

'This is one of your special order cards.'

'Yes, but look what has been written on it.'

She read, '. . . **request the pleasure of Mr and Mrs Robert Burnett Esquire** . . .'

Her face blushed and she exclaimed faintly, 'Robert, us?'

He took hold of her hands.

'Yes, we, my love, are invited to the grand opening of the new dock, to be performed by their Royal Highnesses, the Prince and Princess of Wales.'

'Robert, what an honour! I can't believe it. Pinch me, Robert,' she squealed with delight.

'You, my darling Hannah, have brought me good fortune.'

And he truly believed it as he drew her into his arms and kissed her. Hannah didn't flinch anymore. She had become used to Robert's affectionate ways and responded warmly to him.

The next morning, Hannah was up earlier than she had normally been since her wedding, feeling that she had neglected the Reverend Rendell's soup kitchen. Dressing swiftly so as not to wake Robert, she hurried down the stairs but by the time she had reached the bottom tread a feeling of nausea swept over her. She rushed into the bathroom and when she'd finished being sick, she leaned against the door waiting for the swimming sensation in her head to stop. Then with delicate movements, she scooped up cold water to rinse away the perspiration clogging her eyes and face. Then she dried herself on a rough towel.

In the kitchen, she raked life back into the smouldering hob fire and put the kettle on to boil. A cup of tea and a dry biscuit might settle her stomach. She sighed deeply as she recalled her mother's remedy whenever she had been pregnant. Hannah had recognised the signs, but their significance hadn't registered until now. She let her hands trace over her tummy, feeling nothing but its firmness. Was there really life within her? Tonight she must tell Robert.

Later, having returned home from her stint at the soup kitchen, Hannah decided to go and see her mother's old neighbour, Mrs Binns, who was a nurse-cum-midwife. Filling a basket with tit-bits, she set off for Fretter's Court, near to the Humber Dock.

'Come on in, Hannah. My you do look bonny,' Mrs Binns greeted her, opening the door of her small, terraced house.

Hannah flung herself into the welcoming arms and cuddled the ample figure swathed in her large white apron.

'Sit yourself down,' Mrs Binns said, quickly removing a pile of clean sheets from the well-worn, but comfortable horsehair sofa.

Hannah handed her the laden basket. 'Just a few bits and pieces.'

'You're a kind lass. My brood will soon make short work of this,' she said appreciatively. 'Now let me look at you. Married life suits you. You've got a soft bloom to your cheeks and . . .'

Hannah burst into tears. Mrs Binns

took her once more into her arms.

'Now, don't take on so, lass. I'll make us a pot of tea then you can tell me what's bothering you.'

Mrs Binns ran her expert eye over Hannah and beamed.

'You're with child, aren't you?'

The hot, sweet liquid restored Hannah's wellbeing and she felt much better.

'I'm sorry, Mrs Binns, you must think me a right softy.'

'No, love, a good cry does wonders. It helps to relieve tension and to see things more clearly.'

Hannah smiled weakly.

'I feel much better just talking to you. I do miss Mother so.'

'Of course you do, but life goes on and your mam wouldn't want you to fret.'

Hannah liked Mrs Binns' plain speaking and ventured, 'Mrs Binns, I would like you to deliver my baby.'

'That's as maybe, but your husband might want a doctor in attendance.'

'He doesn't know about the baby yet.'

'My God, lass! You better tell him straight away. You've nothing to hide.'

'I'm telling him tonight. It's just that I wanted to talk to you first, like I would have done with Mam.'

She touched the older woman's arm affectionately.

'You understand, don't you?'

'Aye, lass. Now are you troubled with sickness?'

'Yes.'

'Right.'

Getting to her feet, she reached into the fireside cupboard and selected a small bottle.

'Just a few drops in your morning tea and that'll see you right for the day. Take plenty of fresh air and good food, and when you're a few months gone, make sure you rest in the afternoons.'

That evening, dinner seemed to take for ever. Robert was so full of his plans for the forthcoming royal visit that Hannah could only listen and smile.

Finally he stopped talking and she went with him into his study where he took his port and she occasionally joined him. Now that the moment had come to tell him of her condition she felt nervous. She took a deep breath.

'Robert, you know I love Charlotte dearly, as if she were my own daughter.'

He looked at her over the rim of his glass, giving her his full attention.

'Yes, my dear.'

'Do you ever think of us having children?'

She held her breath, waiting for his reply. What if he didn't want any more children? A terrible thought, but until this moment that hadn't occurred to her. She and Robert had never discussed having children. She watched as he picked up his glass and gulped down the port. Setting the glass carefully on the table he replied in a strained voice.

'What if I was unable to give you children?'

Numbness filled her as she tried to consider his words.

'I don't understand.'

'Hannah, my greatest wish is for us to fill this house with the sound of children's voices. I had a very lonely childhood. I don't wish that for Charlotte.'

Quickly she rose from her chair and went to him, kneeling at his feet as she rested her head on his lap. He stroked her hair soothingly, and then she looked up into his kindly face.

'Robert, I am with child, our child.'

For a moment his eyes were glazed, then he swept her into his arms.

'My sweet Hannah, never leave me.'

She felt his lips feather across hers, trembling as they touched. She would never leave him. She had made her vows. Gently he released her.

'My dear, so Charlotte is to have a brother or sister. This is the most wonderful news.'

His voice broke with emotion, and now it was her turn to hold him close, pleased that she had brought happiness into his life.

The town of Kingston-upon-Hull was now in a state of euphoria. Every time Hannah went into a shop, the main topic of conversation was the royal visit. Robert and businessmen alike discussed that the opening of a new dock would create employment for many.

Hannah walked out with Charlotte and Jenny, admiring the bunting and flags decorating the streets and shops. What money there was to spare was being spent and this in turn generated more money for the shopkeepers who then employed more staff and this led to prosperity for the town.

Even Ruby became intoxicated with the prospect of the royal visit as she chattered to Hannah in the kitchen.

'Fancy, you'll never believe it, but Beeton's in Market Place have three large windows to let for folk to sit in to watch the royal procession go by. Six people at ten shillings each. Who on earth can afford that? Even if I could, I wouldn't pay it, royalty or not,' she concluded indignantly.

Hannah, putting the finishing touches to a batch of fruit pies she was taking along to sell at the chapel bazaar, looked up, feeling guilty.

'I wish Robert could have got more tickets.'

'Don't you fret,' Ruby said. 'We're gonna be all right. It's the promenade for Jenny, little Charlotte and me. There we'll have a grand view of the prince and princess arriving.'

When the great day arrived, the Burnett household was up and about quite early. It seemed to Hannah that no one had slept much that night, the excitement of seeing the royal couple being too much.

Georgie was taking his chances of viewing the royal procession with one of the lads he worked with.

'Hannah, is my hat on straight?' Ruby chirped as she peered in the hallstand mirror.

'Yes, but surely it's too early to be wearing it now.'

'Oh, no! We want a front view on the prom. I've packed a basket of food. Jenny's bringing a rug so Charlotte can have a rest.'

Hannah marvelled at Ruby's organising abilities.

'I'm going upstairs. Let me know when you are going,' she said.

Her room was quiet and peaceful after the state of pandemonium downstairs. Going into Robert's dressing-room, she checked yet again his clothes laid out in readiness for when he returned from his place of business. There was ample time before she needed to dress so she could snatch a rest on the sofa.

No longer did she feel queasy in the mornings, but was often tired in the afternoons and today she wanted to be at her best. She didn't want to miss a single magical moment of seeing a real live prince and princess. She couldn't believe it was happening to her and to be specially invited was indeed an honour. A princess of Danish birth, just like Christian Hansen.

Hannah clasped her hands over her face, sad but not wanting to cry for her lost love, Christian. His memory was still agonisingly sharp.

Hannah Burnett, she scolded herself, be grateful for the blessing you have. You are a married woman expecting a child so it isn't right for you to have fanciful thoughts.

Refreshed after her rest, Hannah began to dress. Standing before her elegant, full-length mirror, she ran her hands over the gentle swell of her stomach. Tucked away inside her the baby was growing though no one would notice yet. She had expertly let out the side seams of her wedding dress and the finished result gave no hint of her thickening waistline.

She didn't hear the bedroom door open and was unaware of Robert entering until he came and stood behind her, his eyes shining with adoration.

'My dear, you are so beautiful and I am so proud of you.'

He kissed the nape of her neck then suddenly she was in his arms.

'Robert,' she whispered. 'You must dress for the royal occasion.'

With a controlled effort he pulled himself away from her.

'Yes, of course, my dear.'

This was their first public engagement together. A few of his fellow acquaintances thought Robert had married beneath himself. In fact it was the reverse. Hannah enriched his life more than anyone would ever know. Each day he thanked the Lord for delivering her to him.

When he was dressed he said to Hannah, 'Close your eyes. I have a surprise for you.'

She felt his hands upon her throat and something touch its hollow.

'Open your eyes.'

She gasped in amazement at the

magnificent necklace of diamonds with a sapphire in the centre.

'But Robert, it's . . . '

'You are my wife. Wear it with pride.'

They alighted from the carriage Robert had hired especially for the occasion at the west end of Wellington Street. The street was crowded with people in jubilant mood and there was cries of admiration as Robert and Hannah walked by. They made a striking couple, Robert handsome with his dark side whiskers, dressed in sombre coat and trousers, with a dash of colour provided by his silk waistcoat, Hannah, by his side, her arm resting lightly on Robert's, her hat newly-trimmed with pale silk violets, which showed off to perfection her luxuriant chestnut hair.

She radiated a warm elegance right down to her feet tucked into her wedding slippers. Added to her ensemble was a parasol, serviceable if the sun shone or if the unthinkable happened, it rained. As they approached the Triumphal Arch especially erected for the occasion, Hannah felt dazzled.

'Robert, look.'

They both paused to gaze at the beautiful design of scroll work and gilt mouldings.

'What does it say?' she asked shading her eyes against the glitter of the gold lettering on a blue satin background.

'God Bless the Prince and Princess,' Robert read proudly.

Swept along by the tide of people, they couldn't linger. Taking their allocated places on the north platform, Hannah glanced around in wonderment. Never in her whole life had she been in the company of so many well-dressed people.

A man with a lady on his arm raised his hat as they passed by and the lady inclined her head with a gracious smile. Robert returned the courtesy and she did the same. Then the man stopped to talk to Robert.

'Well done, sir, excellent work. I shall

write to you accordingly.'

He raised his hat to Hannah then moved on.

Intrigued, Hannah asked, 'What did he mean?'

'It means, my dear, that my business will certainly be expanding and developing.'

She squeezed his arm affectionately. Glancing across to the far aisle she saw Edward Smith-Allen and his wife. He acknowledged her by lifting his hat and she inclined her head in greeting.

By one o'clock, the crowd grew restless when word was passed that the royal procession had been slowed down by the crowds of well-wishers. At a quarter to two, the band struck up and a cheer rose from the spectators. The Prince and Princess of Wales had arrived.

Suddenly the spectators were startled into silence by the sound of gunfire. HMS Dauntless, anchored in the Humber, had begun the twenty-one gun salute and the Artillery and Rifle

Volunteers formed a guard of honour. Hannah held her breath as the royal couple stepped on to the crimson carpet to be received by the local dignitaries and representatives of the Danish inhabitants who had settled in Kingston-upon-Hull.

The Mayor cleared his throat to make the speech of welcome, but the words seemed to waft over Hannah's head for she was quite entranced by the sight of the lovely princess. When the young Danish girl spoke in her native tongue, her words ringing out clear, Hannah listened, catching a word or two that she remembered from when she had first met Christian. Her eyes misted and her thoughts drifted.

Robert touched her arm bringing her back to the present.

'Isn't the princess exquisite?' he whispered.

'She's beautiful,' Hannah replied dreamily, watching as the tall, elegant Princess Alexandra moved gracefully by the side of Prince Edward.

Her dress was a creation of pink satin with a white muslin tunic trimmed with Brussels lace. As the royal couple boarded the HMS Vivid, the Archbishop of York held up his hand to silence everyone while he said a prayer. Then the majestic figure of Edward Prince of Wales stepped into full view. All eyes were upon him. This was the great moment. No one moved. Even the mighty Humber condescended to keep her waters quiet and the gulls sought sanctuary out on the mud flats. The prince spoke in a clear, sonorous voice as he declared, 'I name this dock, Albert Dock.'

At the signal from the Dock Master, the lock gates were opened by the aid of hydraulic power and the HMS Vivid with the royal party aboard sailed forth. Hannah felt almost deafened by the tumultuous cheering.

She herself jumped up and down, most unladylike, as the royal couple waved in their direction. Hannah waved

114

back with her lace handkerchief, as did many other ladies, stopping only when the prince and princess disembarked and entered the luncheon room. Hannah turned to Robert, her face flushed with excitement and happiness.

'Oh, Robert, it's been so wonderful, like a fairytale dream.'

He laughed at her joy.

'A magnificent occasion.'

People began to move forward, making their way out and as the crowd surged, Hannah became separated from Robert. She didn't panic, knowing that they would meet at the exit gate. Suddenly a man stepped in front of her, blocking her way. She waited for him to move, but he didn't.

'Hannah,' the man exclaimed.

Startled by the sound of the voice she looked up into a pair of blue eyes.

'Christian!'

Suddenly she felt faint. People jostled and she was pushed into his arms, strong, tender arms that held her close, steering her away from the path of the moving crowd. It must be an hallucination, caused by the excitement. She tried to look at him again but her vision was blurred. Then he spoke again, in that unmistakable Danish accent.

'You are alone?'

Her mouth dry, she mumbled, 'No.'

Wildly she looked about for Robert, but he was nowhere to be seen. Christian still held her close. He was real.

'Hannah.'

He put a warm hand under her chin. The touch sent a spark of fire through her body and she shimmered with heat.

'You look radiant and so beautiful.'

She found her voice.

'Christian, I thought you were dead. It's a shock to see you.'

His tanned, weathered face beamed at her.

'When the smack floundered I was picked up by another boat en route for Germany. It has taken me months to get home, but I am the lucky one. I was the only survivor.'

'I'm pleased you are sàfe,' she whispered.

'I have only been home two days and I have been sleeping. But I will come to see you, my darling Hannah. Tomorrow I can call, yes?'

Christian, oh, Christian her heart cried with sorrow. It is too late, too late.

'I cannot. I have made a vow,' she whispered.

His head on one side he looked at her.

'A vow? I do not understand what you say.'

She was trying to find the words to answer him when a voice cut into her jumbled thoughts.

'There you are, my dear.'

Robert came between them, taking her arm, and he looked enquiringly at Christian.

Using all the strength she could muster, she said dutifully, 'Robert, this is an old friend of mine, Christian Hansen.'

Robert's face remained bland. He

recognised Christian as the young fisherman whom he had seen with Hannah on the day that he had decided to marry her.

Raising his hat he said politely, 'Good afternoon, a joyous occasion.'

'Yes, indeed,' Christian acknowledged, wondering who the man was whom Hannah was so familiar with.

'You must excuse us, Mr Hansen. With my wife's delicate condition, she tires easily. Come, my dear, our carriage awaits.'

As Robert whisked her away, Hannah threw a glance over her shoulder. Christian's face had turned ashen as he stared after her and she knew by the gaunt expression in his eyes that he felt she had betrayed him. A brutal quirk of fate had robbed her of true love, but she had made a vow and vows could not be broken.

6

Hannah walked slowly from Betchy Chapel through the darkening streets and alleys towards home, each step a struggle. She could feel the baby hanging low in her womb and she knew from her pains its birth was imminent, almost two weeks earlier than the date worked out.

To keep her mind off her labour pains, she thought about the day's happenings. She had spent the cold December day in the soup kitchen, doling out thin, watery soup. Hannah observed that with more tragedies at sea especially amongst the fishing community, the queue of hungry people, mostly women and children, became longer.

Taking their cue from the Reverend Rendell, the helpers acted in a dignified manner. Somehow, despite their plight, the hungry women demanded it. It was bad enough having to accept charity knowing that they couldn't care for their children. Sympathy, they did not need. Though poor, they had their pride. Hannah recalled her dear mother's words, 'Never lose your pride and hold your head up high.'

When times had been bad for Hannah, she had adhered to that philosophy, and now, Robert was supportive of her good work, taking great delight in mentioning it to his new business acquaintance.

He now devoted long hours to his now prosperous business. Soon he would be in a position to buy his own carriage, not that she begrudged him this because he worked so hard. It was her inadequacy she bemoaned, wishing that she could do more to help the bereaved families of the smackmen. Although her life was quite comfortable now, she had never forgotten her roots.

She winced as another kicking pain gripped her. The baby wanted to make its presence known. Dear God, she prayed, let me get home in time. By the time she entered the house in Arden Square, she was in a state of collapse. Ruby took charge of the situation, bawling out orders.

'Jenny, help me get her upstairs. Georgie, run for Mrs Binns.'

Once on her bed, Hannah couldn't contain her screams of agony.

'Oh, no! Don't have it yet, Hannah,' Ruby panicked. 'I know nowt about bringing babies into the world.'

'I want plenty of hot water,' a brisk voice said.

Mrs Binns had arrived!

Less than one hour later, the bedroom was filled with the lusty cries of a new-born infant. John Robert Burnett had made his way into the world on the last day of the year.

'Here he is,' Mrs Binns cooed as she placed the baby, wrapped in a clean white sheet, into Hannah's arms.

Hannah's eyes glistened like sunlight on calm waters as she gazed down on her sleeping son. Tracing her fingers over his soft, pink skin she marvelled at the abundant tufts of chestnut hair, the same colour as hers.

Putting her little finger in the tiny fist of her son's hand, she exclaimed, 'Mrs Binns, he's wonderful. So perfect.'

She hugged him close, loving the smell of his warm body.

'He is that, Hannah, luv,' the midwife declared.

There was a tap on the door and Ruby entered bearing a tea tray.

'The master wants to know when he can come up,' she asked.

'In about half-an-hour we'll be ready for him,' Mrs Binns replied.

Ruby's eyes strayed to where Hannah lay in bed cradling the baby.

'May I have a peep?'

'Just a quick one,' Mrs Binns replied. 'I must get Hannah looking bonny for her husband.'

'My, he's so tiny,' Ruby marvelled, and looking at Hannah, unashamed tears coursed down her flushed cheeks.

Robert entered the room quietly surprised to see Hannah sitting up in bed. He could only stand and stare in admiration. She had taken the trouble to change into a clean cotton night-gown trimmed with lace and her hair was brushed to a brilliant shine. He drew nearer, bewitched by the soft beauty that glowed from his young wife. Instinctively he bent forward and kissed her warm lips.

Shyly Hannah asked, 'What do you think of our son, Robert?'

His hands, though big, were gentle as he touched the velvet cheeks of his son's face.

'He's beautiful.'

A lump struck in his throat. His voice low and emotional he continued.

'Hannah, my darling wife, you have brought me such happiness. I am truly blessed. I give thanks to God.'

Just then Mrs Binns entered the room and touched his arm.

'I think she needs to rest now, sir.'

Downstairs in his study, Robert

poured himself a brandy and sat down by the fireside and watched the colourful flames dance. He must have fallen asleep for a loud knock on the door awoke him. He glanced at the mantelpiece clock and saw it was past midnight, the first day of the New Year. He shook his head free of slumber.

'Enter,' he called.

It was Fanny, one of the new maids. She bobbed a curtsey.

'If yer please, sir, it's madam.'

He sprang to his feet nearly knocking the girl over.

'My wife? What's wrong?'

Fanny, overawed by his reaction, took a few steps back and bobbed another curtsey.

'If yer please, sir, she just wants to see yer.'

Quickly she moved to one side as he rushed from the room. She followed him into the hall, staring as he bounded up the staircase, two steps at a time. The bedroom door was slightly ajar and for a moment he stood listening, expecting to hear the sound of panic within, but there was nothing. Cautiously he tapped on the door and slowly opened it wider. Hannah was sitting up in bed and the baby, his precious son, was suckling at her breast.

Hannah saw him and noticed the hesitation on his face. She smiled at him, her face aglow.

'Come closer, Robert,' she whispered.

He didn't know what to say to her, but then there didn't seem the need for words. He sat on the edge of the bed and watched as the contented infant took his fill. Never had he seen such a wonderful sight. His first wife had banned him from these occasions.

After the feed, Hannah made the baby comfortable, and then she smiled shyly at Robert.

'Would you like to hold him?' she asked tenderly.

'But I might drop him.'

He looked at the fragile bundle nestling in Hannah's arms and he felt so big and clumsy. She held John out to him.

'He'll be quite safe.'

Tenderly he nursed the soft, warm infant in his arms, mesmerised by the well-formed features of his son's face. Holding him close he could feel the tiny heartbeat of his son and tears of joy filled his eyes.

'He's so perfect. I cannot believe he is mine — ours,' he corrected.

He gazed adoringly at Hannah.

'Our son, John Robert Burnett,' he acclaimed proudly.

He was touched that Hannah had agreed on his father's name for their son. John stirred in Robert's arms, stretching his body then drawing up his little legs to touch his chest.

'Amazing, Hannah, look.'

But Hannah, her mane of chestnut hair fanned out on the soft, feathery pillow was fast asleep. Robert didn't panic but laid John down in his crib. He looked from sleeping mother to sleeping son and a great surge of love and contentment filled him to the brim.

Crossing over to the window, he drew aside the drapes and gazed out. Snow lay as soft as a carpet of pure white wool. Inside the glow from the fire flitted round the room like sunlight dancing on a summer's day. The only sounds in the room were the rhythmic tick of the clock on the dresser, the gentle breathing of his wife and a low intermittent murmur from his son.

He sat down on the chair by the bed and when Fanny came to take up her position by her mistress's side, Robert sent her away. He wanted to spend these most precious hours just watching over his wife and son.

★ ★ ★

Tom Cullen took great delight in telling Christian Hansen that his sister, Hannah, had given birth to a son. Christian's reaction was to say he was pleased and wished mother and son well, but that evening he went to the

127

dockside beerhouse and supped ale until his mind became so fuddled he could no longer think.

Next day, making his way to the new Albert Dock, Christian tried to erase thoughts of Hannah from his mind. Reaching the dock, his heart soared at the sight of the sleek body of his fishing smack, the Indigo. Pride shone on his rugged, tanned face. He would soon set off on his first trip as skipper of his own craft. He had fulfilled his dream, but sadly not with Hannah by his side. He knew now that he had taken her too much for granted.

It took him only two days to assemble a willing crew and stock up with provisions. The Indigo sailed on the early-morning tide with Christian determined to seek a great catch. He made for the North Sea, knowing the weather conditions would be rough with bitter, cold winter winds, which would bring snow and freezing ice, but his crew was a hardy bunch, well used to enduring the harsh, working environment and they would have the pleasing incentive of extra money to jingle in their pockets.

★　★　★

Two months after John was born, Hannah engaged a young girl to help Jenny with the children and she returned to helping out at the chapel soup kitchen. Usually she was home in the afternoon, but after yet another fishing tragedy she had seen the way the women and children hung around the chapel. Her heart went out to them. She would often stand talking to them and in doing so she found out that the majority of the women wished that they had work to do to earn enough money to support their families otherwise they were going to end up in the workhouse.

Hannah remembered that fear only too well because it had been her mother's. But they had been fortunate. Edward Smith-Allen had been her father's employer and he was generous to them. Hannah believed that was because George Cullen had been a good fisherman, but some neighbours made unpleasant insinuations about her mother's friendship with him.

By the summer, Hannah found premises to rent quite close to Arden Square. Once an old bakery but now neglected, dirty, damp, she set to work and with the help of the fishermen's widows they scrubbed it out, repaired windows and doors. Then she walked with pride from room to room absorbing the fragrant freshness of lavender water. In the kitchen, Hannah stopped to inspect the old oven, its door hanging from a broken hinge.

'If we could repair the oven, we could bake our own bread,' she enthused to Maisie, a thin, but warm-hearted woman who clung to her side.

'Our Ted could fix it, miss.'

Ted, Maisie's eldest son, managed to procure a replacement hinge for the oven. Maisie put herself in charge of baking and at first she baked just enough bread for their needs. Then Hannah suggested that if they baked a few extra loaves they could sell them and then buy material and trimmings to start up a workshop.

Hannah made the soup, but she really wanted to provide more variety of foods. Ruby sent her now-famous fruit loaves, but that would only be short term. Although Robert, so busy with his business, didn't object to her good work, he didn't expect her to finance it from his own household.

One day, needing someone to talk to about her project, Hannah called on the Reverend Rendell.

'I want so much to provide more support for the fishing families. I want to help them to become more self-sufficient. It's so frustrating, the lack of funds.'

They sat in his office, drinking tea.

'What you need, Mrs Burnett, is an assistant.'

'But how could I pay an assistant?' she asked wearily.

'You have upstairs rooms at the premises?'

'Yes.'

'They could become living quarters for your assistant in lieu of wages. I think I may have the very person for you.'

The next day Hannah called at the chapel to meet the woman who would become her assistant. Miss Amy Nightingale was a woman of small independent means, in her late twenties. Plainly dressed, but expensive cloth, her neat green gown was edged with a white lace collar. There was an air of gentleness about her and from beneath the brim of her bonnet a pair of grey eyes stared apprehensively at Hannah.

Hannah's first impression was that this woman wouldn't enjoy working with the often rough, but proud fishing folk. But Hannah didn't have a choice. She needed help desperately. She stretched a smile on her tired face and held out her hand.

In fact, Amy Nightingale proved to be just what Hannah required.

'You need more money, Mrs Burnett. I will write to all the local businessmen and traders for financial help and maybe their wives will organise charity events to raise funds.'

Amy settled into the upstairs rooms with help from Maisie and Ted. She brought along her own bed, a desk, a comfortable chair and a rug, and Hannah provided drapes and linen. One evening Hannah invited her to dinner to meet Robert, but after the introductions and a few spoken niceties Robert seemed to be preoccupied with his own thoughts.

While Hannah set up the workshop for the women, Amy used the backroom as a schoolroom for the children. With the money earned from selling the extra loaves of bread to the corner shop, Hannah trawled the market stalls for second-hand clothes, which could be repaired and made use of. Two of the women snipped off buttons from old garments and Hannah sold the buttons on to the nearby sewing factory.

She also obtained off-cuts of card and vellum, trimming them to the size of calling cards, which were decorated with pretty flower designs by Meg and her four daughters. Hannah would watch Meg, who sat at the table nearest the window to catch the light, holding a small sable-haired artist's brush in her big rough hands. Amazingly, Hannah thought, she watched as Meg produced delicate, intricate works of art.

When the calling cards were finished, Mr Adams, a friendly bookseller agreed to sell them, taking a small percentage from each sale. Hannah's hopes were high that one day, in the not-too-distant future, the refuge, now referred to as Hope House, would be self-sufficient.

Amy had visited all the dames' schools in the area and managed to procure from each a slate or two. And now the older children, sitting crossed legged on the scrubbed, wooden floor, wrote with their slate pencils, copying the text she'd written on the board in her beautiful, copperplate handwriting.

Late one afternoon, Hannah had made a pot of tea and Amy joined her in the walk-in cupboard they used as an office. As she poured, it occurred to Hannah that she didn't really know anything about Amy's background.

'Amy, forgive me for asking and pray do not answer if you do not wish. I was just wondering why someone of your breeding and status would want to work with the poor of the fishing community.'

Amy sipped her tea thoughtfully then put her cup firmly on the saucer.

'I was an embarrassment to my family. My father died and my brother inherited the family estate, taking care of my mother. I was engaged to marry a neighbouring landowner when he suddenly decided to marry a far richer lady. All I have is a small allowance from the estate. My brother said he couldn't afford to keep me so I found work as a governess, but I wasn't suited. Then my friend the Reverend Rendell came to my rescue. The rest you know.'

Hannah placed her hand affectionately on Amy's arm.

'Amy, you came to my rescue. Without you, how could I possibly run the refuge? You've done wonders with the children and raising funds. We are a team. Now, let's have another cup of tea and a slice of Ruby's cake.'

By the time she reached Arden Square that evening, Hannah was exhausted, but she always looked forward to bathing the children and reading them a bedtime story. Usually by the time she had tucked the children into bed, Robert was home and he would come up and kiss them goodnight. Then they would have dinner together, but tonight he was late yet again.

She looked at her sleeping children and her heart fluttered with love for them. Now Hope House was becoming more established, she intended to take off one day a week to devote just to her children, especially now the warm summer days were here.

Ruby was flapping in the kitchen.

'If I don't serve dinner soon, it'll be ruined,' she moaned.

Hannah felt too upset to pacify her. Usually Robert sent word with Georgie he was going to be late. She paced the hall quietly fuming, feeling the tension building within her. Suddenly the front door rattled and she wrenched it open.

'Robert!'

She was just about to let out a tirade but when she saw his weary face and hunched shoulders, she checked herself.

Instead she helped him off with his coat.

'Sorry, Hannah, I should have sent a message but I didn't realise it was so late. Are the children asleep?'

'Yes, Robert, they have been asleep for quite some time.'

She winced when she saw the hurt expression on his face. She offered a smile, saying pleasantly, 'You can have a peep at them later. Would you like to change before dinner?'

'No, but I would like a drink first.'

She slipped her arm through his and led him into the dining-room. Something was wrong, she could sense it. She poured Robert a large brandy, then waited for the maid to leave the room.

'Robert, is there something wrong?'

He drained his goblet, staring at its emptiness before he spoke.

'It's been a most trying day. I've just left my banker.'

His eyes were downcast. She was surprised. Usually he didn't like to discuss money matters with her.

Wearily, he rose from his chair and went over to the sideboard and refilled his goblet with brandy and drank it immediately. Hannah was speechless. She'd never seen Robert do such a thing before.

He didn't move but just stared at her. 'I'm afraid I have bad news.'

7

Hannah sat very still, Robert's words reverberating in her head — bad news, bad news. Her hand clutching at her throat she moaned silently. Was it her brother, Tom? Had there been another smack lost at sea? Then her eyes became wide with horror — Christian?

Her voice a thin wail she cried, 'Robert, tell me please, I beseech you.'

Suddenly he was by her side.

'My darling Hannah, do not upset yourself so.'

She grabbed frantically at his jacket.

'Tell me the worst.'

He freed himself from her grasp.

'Only if you promise to stay calm.'

She stared at him, mortified. How could she stay calm if the man she loved was declared dead yet again? It was more than her heart could take.

Robert sighed heavily and went over

to the sideboard and poured out two brandies, giving Hannah one.

'Drink this, my dear.'

The golden liquid slipped down her throat like molten fire, steadying her inner tremor, giving her a small degree of composure. Clasping her hands tightly together on her lap, she faced Robert, now seated, and waited for him to speak. His voice was barely audible.

'Earlier this year I invested money in what seemed to be a profitable deal, but the investment has collapsed and I have lost all the money. I am ruined, Hannah, ruined.'

Unable to endure the confused look in her eyes, he let his head slump forward. She could only gape at the dejected figure of her husband in utter bewilderment. What was he talking about? Why didn't he tell her the bad news? She pushed back her chair and seized the lapels of his jacket, her voice almost hysterical.

'Robert, for goodness' sake, tell me what the tragedy is.'

Stupefied, he stared at his wife. Never before had he seen her in such a wild state. The brandy, he thought, I shouldn't have given it to her.

Seeing that she wasn't getting any sense from Robert by being angry she took a deep breath and spoke calmly.

'The bad news, is it Tom? Is he dead?'

She couldn't bring herself to say Christian's name.

Realisation hit Robert.

'My darling, no one is dead, least of all your brother. The bad news is my business. I have lost nearly all my money.'

'But I don't understand. You are a prosperous businessman.'

He explained as patiently as he could about the investment plan that was going to make him richer than ever. When he had finished, Hannah nodded that she understood, but she didn't really. It still wasn't clear to her how the money could just disappear. What concerned her more was the devastating effect this was having on Robert as once again he slumped in his chair. All thoughts of Christian Hansen had gone from her head.

A knock on the dining-room door heralded the maid with a pot of freshly-brewed coffee. She stared at the uneaten dessert and then at the slumped figure of her master.

'You may clear away later,' Hannah said, her voice not betraying the bewilderment she felt.

She poured coffee and placed a cup before Robert.

'Drink this. It may help to clear your head.'

She put her arm around his shoulders to comfort him and felt him trembling.

'Do you want to talk more?' she asked, not sure how to help him.

He shook his head. She watched him sip his coffee, a vacant expression in his eyes and she wondered what was in his mind.

Robert knew he had been a fool. If only he had followed his own rules, his own instincts instead of trusting to others. Work hard, stick to what he knew, had until then proved to be successful. Why, oh, why did he listen to that cad, Huntington? He had thought he could dabble with money, show the world he, Robert Burnett, successful businessman, was not frightened to take a chance. How naïve! Now his only salvation was to save what he could. He glanced across at his wife, his beloved, trusting, innocent Hannah. He had failed her. He spoke his thoughts out loud.

'I did it for our son, John. I wanted to secure his future,' he breathed, and to his utter dismay uncontrollable tears coursed down his cheeks.

'Oh, Robert.'

Forgetting her own feelings, Hannah flung her arms about Robert and held him close, soothing him like she would a child. For a full ten minutes, which seemed more like ten hours, she held him close. Finally quiet, he untangled himself from her and lifting up his head, his red-rimmed, sunken eyes stared at her. His voice shook as he struggled with words.

'Forgive me, Hannah. I am a grown man. I shouldn't be displaying such signs of weakness.'

'I am your wife and I am here to comfort and support you,' she replied with a confidence she didn't feel.

'Thank you, my dear.'

He patted her hand, sighing heavily.

'Hopefully I can retain the shop.'

'What about the printing works?'

He looked away from her. It hurt to see her beautiful, honey-coloured eyes darken at the prospect of an uncertain future.

The following Sunday morning, after another restless night, Hannah awoke earlier to find Robert had already left the bed. She slipped a wrap over her cotton nightgown and went downstairs to the kitchen and made a pot of tea, taking it along to the study. Robert was sitting at his desk sorting through papers and ledgers, growing more and more agitated.

Placing the tray on the occasional table, unable to see him so distressed, she asked, 'Can I help you, Robert?'

Without looking up he retorted, 'How can a woman help?'

Hannah bit her lip and refrained from remarking at his bad manner. She poured out the tea and handed him a cup.

'Sorry, I didn't mean to snap,' he said, trying to keep his voice level.

He gave her a pinched smile and picked up the cup, but his hand shook so much it spilled on to the rug at his feet. He stared down at the dark brown liquid, its rivulets staining the fawn-patterned rug.

Glad of a reason to leave the room, Hannah said, 'I'll fetch a cloth.'

The second she went, Robert pushed back his chair. Avoiding the mess, he moved with short, jerky steps to the wine table. On the tray were a decanter of port and one of brandy. Stealthily he poured out a large goblet of brandy, telling himself that at this time of the morning it was purely for medicinal purposes. He gulped it down in one go. When Hannah returned he was quite composed.

'My dear, I must go to the shop. I need to check the stock.'

'But it's Sunday, Robert,' she exclaimed surprised, knowing that they always went to church for the morning service.

His manner was apologetic as he replied.

'I'm sorry, my dear, but it is necessary.'

'If you must go, take Georgie. An extra pair of hands will make the work lighter. I can come to the shop later and bring you a bite to eat if you send the carriage back for me.'

He stood up, towering over her.

'I've sold the carriage,' he said bluntly.

Hannah escaped to the kitchen, glad

of the warmth. Keeping her voice light she spoke to Ruby.

'Good morning. I've come to make up a basket of food for Georgie and Robert.'

News must travel fast as Ruby said, 'I heard they're going to work. Fancy, on a Sunday. Is summat up?'

Hannah would dearly have liked to confide in Ruby, but there was no sense in alarming her with talk of lost money and its consequences.

'They've something urgent to attend to.'

Changing the subject she inspected the cakes baking in the oven.

'They smell good, Ruby.'

'Sit yourself down. You can have a hot, buttered one, with preserve.'

She fussed round Hannah, aware of the troubled look in her eyes.

Later that morning, Hannah walked to Robert's shop in Market Place. She would have liked the children to come with her but under the circumstances she didn't think it was wise. She promised Charlotte she would take her for a walk to the pier in the afternoon when John was having his nap.

She prayed she didn't meet anyone she knew because she wouldn't know what to say to them, not sure if Robert's predicament was common knowledge. At last, she sighed with relief as she reached the shop, the laden basket now weighing heavily on her arm. She looked up at the boldly painted sign displayed above the bow window: ROBERT BURNETT & SON.

Tears filled Hannah's eyes as she remembered Robert's pride on the completion of the new sign the week after John was born. Such a happy day it had been and now . . . Shuddering, she fixed a smile on her face and entered the shop. Georgie was perched on the midway rung of a ladder searching in the corners of darkened shelves for boxes of long-forgotten stationery items. Robert, his face streaked with dust, was making entries in a huge brown ledger. On seeing

Hannah, he laid down his quill, flexing his stiff fingers, glad of a break from his unenviable task. She placed the basket on one of the counters and Georgie jumped down from the ladder.

'I'm famished, Hannah,' he said, lifting a corner of the checked cloth covering the food and sniffing appreciatively. 'By heck, it smells good.'

At any other time she would have told him to wash his sticky, dirty hands, but not today. She wasn't certain if Robert had told him about the loss of money, but he would have guessed that something was wrong. Georgie's eagerness to eat coupled with his grinning wide looks warmed Hannah's heart. Even Robert's appetite was ravenous, but he offered no conversation.

She stayed less than an hour sensing that Robert wanted her gone.

'Try not to be too late, Robert. The children . . .'

But he was not listening to her.

Outside on the pavement she took a deep breath to steady herself and as she did so she caught the whiff of salty air and fish. A catch landed on a Sunday wouldn't meet with the approval of the strict nonconformists. She hadn't been down to the docks since the grand opening by the Prince and Princess of Wales. Suddenly an overwhelming desire to see the fish dock filled her. Absurd, she thought, but the feeling wouldn't go away, and instinctively her steps took her in the direction of Albert Dock.

As she neared the dock she could see the masts and rigs of boats silhouetted against the strong cobalt-blue sky and her heartbeat quickened. Idly she glanced about. For a Sunday the dock was quite busy with a number of men working, unloading cargo and some just loafing around. As she sauntered along the quayside she realised just how much she had missed the hustle and bustle of the docks.

Turning a corner she came upon a completely different scene, like stepping back in time to her childhood. It was a scene that had scarred her life and ended her childhood. Before her now stood a small group of silent, ill-clad women. She felt out of place in her best Sunday dress of fine blue wool and was just about to move on.

'I know you,' one of the women said. 'You're Mrs Burnett from Hope House.'

Hannah looked into the sad grey eyes of a thin, scraggy-looking woman with three young children clinging to her torn skirt.

'Yes, I am. You are?'

'Lizzie Trotter. I'm waiting for my man. He'll be coming in soon. They say he's gone, but he ain't. He's coming home. He can't leave me now.'

Her pitiful voice filled the air and her children began to cry. Hannah could see that she was pregnant. She put out an arm to comfort Lizzie, but the woman knocked it off in an aggressive manner.

'Keep yer hands off me, Lady Muck.'

Startled by her outburst, Hannah stepped back.

'Take no notice of her, missus,' a small tubby woman said. 'She's not right in the head. She lost her man months ago and she's always down here.'

'I'm sorry,' Hannah said. 'Are you waiting for a smack?'

'The Allen Ho. It should have been back by now. The last we heard they'd gone to German waters, hoping for a good catch.'

The woman's voice trembled.

'Allen Ho? Isn't that one of Mr Smith-Allen's boats?'

Hannah looked round the dock expecting to see him.

'Aye, but he ain't here. He's just buried his wife. Fever, they say she died of, and he's laid low. Lord knows what'll happen to us if he goes.'

Hannah stayed chatting to the women, but there was still no sign of the Allen Ho. Remembering her promise to Charlotte, she was anxious to get back home.

'I have to go now, but I'm at Hope House tomorrow. If you need any help come and see me.'

'Thanks, missus.'

By the time Hannah reached Arden Square, it was raining hard and she was soaked. Quickly changing into dry clothes she went along the corridor to the nursery. John was having his nap and Charlotte was sulking.

'Don't like you, Mama,' she pouted. 'You've made it rain.'

Hannah spoke quietly to Jenny and her young helper.

'Go down and have your afternoon tea. I'll stay with the children.'

From the bookshelf Hannah chose Charlotte's favourite storybook. Going up to her daughter, for she was hers in every sense, she said softly, 'Come, my darling, and sit on my knee. I will read to you.'

Hannah sat on a low chair and Charlotte, who needed no second bidding, clambered on to her lap and snuggled up. Later, when Jenny came back into the nursery, she found both Hannah and Charlotte fast asleep. John lay in his crib, wide awake, cooing happily.

The next day, Robert had left the house long before Hannah was up. She saw to the household and had breakfast with the children. Holding John in her arms, she was reluctant to put him down. He was such a pleasant baby and she loved him dearly but, she sighed, Hope House needed her. Her consolation was she could go knowing that her children would be well cared for. On arriving at Hope House she was met by Maisie.

'Won't be able to sell many loaves today. Allen Ho is lost with all hands.'

'Oh, no,' Hannah gasped, thinking of the poor women she'd seen yesterday.

Their wait had been in vain. A rage blew up within her. The sea would never change its ways so why didn't man provide safer working conditions? She, a mere woman, could see the logic of this. Rolling up her sleeves she set to work in the kitchen. In times of stress, food was a great comforter.

The year progressed and Robert hung on to his shop with only him and Georgie running it. They worked long hours and Hannah rarely saw Robert. Their time together became less. He took to drinking alone in his study of an evening or he would visit his club to escape, but that proved to be a disaster as they snubbed him, the very same men who only a short time ago were happy doing business with him. Unable to hold his head up high he then sought solace in drinking in beerhouses, mixing with riff-raff who'd listen to any story for the price of ale.

Unbeknown to Hannah, many was the night that Georgie, now a strongly-built lad, found Robert drunk in the gutter and brought him home. Then one night Robert was brought home with a gash in his forehead and Dr Johnson had to be sent for. The next morning, Robert insisted on going to the shop, but Hannah was firm.

'No, Robert, today you stay in bed and I will take care of you.'

She made him beef tea and several tasty morsels, and while he slept, she watched over him, studying his face. His once-firm cheeks were now red and puffy and flesh sagged from his lower jaw. Hannah's spirits plummeted. In a few short months her husband's health had deteriorated rapidly. But she managed to keep him at home for a few days and he seemed to be behaving quite normally again. He played with the children and he and Hannah resumed having their evening meal together and she would read to him of an evening, to distract his thoughts.

After a week, he returned to the shop and Hannah to Hope House. She began to return home via the shop and walk with Robert, snuggling together under the umbrella sheltering from the winter rain. This euphoria continued until one day at Hope House just as they were closing for the night, a fight broke out.

'Hannah, Hannah,' a terrified Amy called as she cowered in the tiny office.

Lizzie Trotter had pinched a warm, woollen scarf from a newcomer, Mary Tate, and Mary was demanding it back. Lizzie punched Mary on the chin and Mary retaliated by kicking Lizzie on the shin. As the fight graduated to hair pulling, pandemonium broke out, their children hiding under a table screaming with fear.

By the time Hannah appeased the two women and soothed their children, then made Amy a cup of sweet tea for her nerves, it was quite late. But nevertheless Hannah hurried to the shop, only to find it closed. Out of breath, she leaned against the wall for support. Had Robert gone straight home? Wearily she turned for Arden Square, glancing in beerhouses as she passed by, but she saw no sign of Robert, so he must be home.

It was a cold, January night and she

was glad to open the door at Arden Square and feel the warmth of the house.

'Robert,' she called. 'I'm home.'

There was no reply. She went into the study but he wasn't there, nor was he in their room. Quickly she went to the nursery. The children had had their baths and were tucked up in their beds, fast asleep.

'Have you seen Mr Burnett?' she asked Jenny.

'Not tonight.'

She went downstairs into the kitchen.

'You're home then,' Ruby said. 'This duck'll spoil if I keep it any longer.'

'Have you seen Mr Burnett?'

Ruby looked up from straining vegetables.

'Ain't he with you?'

'No. I was late getting away and when I went to the shop he'd gone.'

'Well, Georgie's home. He's had his tea and gone to rest.'

Slowly Hannah climbed the stairs to her room, knowing in her heart that

158

Robert had slipped back into his old ways of frequenting the beerhouses. What could she do? He was a grown man, who worked so hard for his family. His only fault had been to be too trusting where money was concerned. Now he suffered the consequences, and because Robert considered himself a failure, so they all suffered.

In her bedroom, she undressed and sat at her dressing-table and began to brush her hair with the silver hairbrush Robert had given her as a wedding present. She looked at her pale reflection in the mirror and wondered what she could do to help Robert overcome his anxiety.

After a while she got into bed and lay listening to the sounds of the house, waiting for Robert to come home. Hearing the clock in the drawing-room chime twelve, she flung back the bedclothes and padded across to the window. Pulling back the curtains she gazed down on the empty square.

Throwing a shawl about her shoulders she hurried up to Georgie's room and roused him.

'What's up?' he asked sleepily.

'Robert hasn't come home.'

Georgie struggled into his pants and laced up his boots.

'I'll find him. Don't worry.'

Hannah went into the kitchen and put a log on the smouldering fire and made a pot of strong coffee. Robert would need it. About an hour later she heard the sound of the front door opening and she jumped up. Thank goodness, he's home, she thought rushing into the hall. But Georgie was alone.

'Where is he?'

Exhausted, Georgie said, 'I've searched everywhere. He ain't about.'

In the kitchen they both drank the black coffee. It was going to be a long night, but they drifted into sleep only to be woken by a loud knocking on the front door. It was Ruby who answered the door, to a police constable.

'Is Mrs Burnett at home?'

Hannah came into the hall, pulling her shawl closer around her.

'I'm Mrs Burnett.'

'I think you'd better sit down, madam.'

Ruby took hold of her arm and guided her to a chair. Hannah floated in a daze. Her mouth opened but no words would come. The constable stood awkwardly and stared straight ahead.

'Mrs Burnett, it is my painful duty to inform you that Mr Robert Burnett's body was fished out of the dock an hour ago and awaits your formal identification.'

Hannah heard someone screaming inside her head and then darkness hit her as she slipped into oblivion.

8

It was the Reverend Rendell who identified Robert's body. Hannah was in such a state of shock that Ruby sent for Dr Johnson. He administered a sleeping draught and she sank into a fretful sleep.

Foul play was not suspected. It seemed that Robert had missed his footing and had fallen into the dock. According to the landlord of the Seven Stars Tavern, he was drunk, refusing offers of help to see him home safely.

Hannah could not come to terms with her tragedy.

'He had me and the children to live for,' she said tearfully to her sister, Lily, who had come to comfort her.

Since the death of her mother which had forced them into the orphanage, Hannah's desire to have all her siblings together had not been possible. Ironically, with the death of Robert, they were now all together, united in grief. At the funeral, Georgie, Tom and Lily flanked Hannah. She was glad of their support as they followed Robert's coffin down the aisle of Betchy Street Chapel.

A heavy veil covered her pale face and her beautiful chestnut hair was hidden beneath a black feathered hat. She moved as if she walked on water, but she held her head high, for Robert's sake.

Edward Smith-Allen had sent his carriage for her use, such a kind offer from a man beset with his own worries. Her biggest surprise was seeing Christian Hansen at the funeral, but she didn't get to talk to him. Perhaps people weren't as against Robert as he had feared. Her eyes filled with tears. Her dear husband who had always been so caring was no more.

In the house at Arden Square, Hannah finally broke down, sobbing on to Lily's shoulder, 'What will I do without Robert?'

Lily patted her sister sympathetically. 'You have John and Charlotte.'

And, Lily thought to herself, you've got this big house and servants. You got more than me.

The following week, young Mr Block of Block, Block & Kemp, Solicitors, called to see her. She received him in the drawing-room. To the man sat opposite her, she appeared composed as she poured tea from an elegant silver teapot and offered him a piece of fruit loaf.

'Liquidation!'

She repeated the word the solicitor had just pronounced. She wasn't sure what it meant, but it sounded an ugly, frightening word. Joshua Block fingered his side-whiskers.

'Nothing to alarm yourself about. The shop and contents will have to be sold to pay off Mr Burnett's outstanding debts.'

'I see,' Hannah said, her voice giving no hint of the rising panic she felt.

'What about the house?'

'You are fortunate. The house is safe. Once the business is disposed of and the creditors paid, there should be sufficient money for you to run your household, though on more modest lines.'

He smiled, and rose to take his leave.

'As soon as the business is completed, I will contact you, Mrs Burnett.'

'Thank you, Mr Block,' she replied politely as he left.

For some time after Robert's death, Hannah confined herself to the house. The trees in the square wore soft green leaves, but for Hannah the coming of spring slipped by unnoticed. She left Amy to run Hope House while she devoted herself to spending time with John and Charlotte and attending to household matters. Ruby proved quite capable of managing the house with the help of Fanny.

Jenny loved Charlotte and John, becoming quite upset thinking she would have to leave, but Hannah reassured her she could stay. Georgie found employment with a printing firm and contributed to the household budget. Hannah began to feel redundant and found too much idle time made her remorseful.

Seeking out Ruby in the kitchen one day, Hannah declared, 'Tomorrow I shall return to help those less fortunate than me.'

'About time,' Ruby mused. 'You're forever in my way.'

Next morning, feeling the renewed vigour of her calling, Hannah was preparing to leave the house when an unexpected visitor arrived. Standing in the cold drawing-room she waited impatiently by the unlit fire to receive Edward Smith-Allen. As he entered the room she drew in a sharp intake of breath, appalled by the deterioration in his appearance. Once a tall man he now stooped, his once-dark hair was sparse and white, and his grey skin was tinged yellow. Quickly she pulled out a chair for him.

'Sit down. May I offer you a brandy?'

He waved a feeble hand.

'You are so kind to one who has done you a great injustice,' he said rather abruptly.

She looked at him sharply, not understanding the meaning of his words and wondered if he was suffering a fever.

'Do you need a doctor?'

'No! I am soon to be delivered into the hands of another.'

Hannah felt uneasy as she handed him the glass of brandy. His fingers touched hers, ice cold. Her irritation at the delay in her return to Hope House abated slightly, but she remained standing.

'How may I help you?'

Edward gulped down the brandy, sensing her impatience.

'I'll come straight to the point. I'm terminally ill, I haven't long to live.'

He watched her closely. Her hand fluttered, her face quivered slightly, but that was all. What had he expected?

'I'm sorry, Mr Smith-Allen,' she said, and she truly was, but why was he here?

'It's your son, John, I've come to discuss.'

Suddenly she was alert.

'John? Why?'

He leaned back in his chair, his face softening.

'First, I'll tell you a story of the woman I truly loved. She was governess to my two young sisters, and most nights we would be together. Our daughter was conceived in love, bringing us to the brink of happiness. Then . . .'

Tears filled his eyes, coursing down his cheeks.

Alarmed by his distress she went to his side.

'Mr Smith-Allen, don't upset yourself. I didn't know you had a daughter.'

'My parents made me give up my love and our daughter. They sent me away and banished my love from the house.'

'I'm sorry. What became of them?'

she asked politely.

'By the time I found where she had gone, it was too late. She'd married another man and he gave my daughter his name.'

'How cruel.'

And sad, she thought, that he had lived his life childless without his daughter.

'Did your mother ever speak of me?' he asked plaintively.

'My mother!'

Her mind flashed back to her mother's last illness when often she would call out the name, Edward, and she also recalled the gossip from the other fishermen's wives.

He didn't wait for her answer.

'She wouldn't take a shilling from me, she was so proud. But I made sure George Cullen always had work.'

Hannah paled and turned to stare unseeingly out of the window, her heart beating rapidly. Then she spun round.

'What was your true love's name?'

His face broke into a smile.

'Why, Ellen, of course, your mother. I loved her with all my heart.'

Hannah's whole body trembled as she asked, 'And your daughter's name?'

'Come here, my child.'

Compelled, she went to him as he reached out.

'My mother would have loved you. You are her image. How sad she never knew you.'

A faraway look crept into his eyes. Hannah pulled away and went to pour herself a brandy, offering him another, but he declined.

'I must talk to you about John, my grandson.'

Stark horror etched her face and her hands clenched into fists.

'John is mine. You can't take him away from me.'

'Dear Hannah, no need for alarm. Soon I will meet my maker and be reunited with Ellen. Before I do I need to make my peace with you. You and John are my only kin. What of John's future?'

She shot him a sharp glance. What could she say? All Robert's dreams for his son had vanished.

'Your only asset is this house and a small income?' he went on.

She drew herself up proudly.

'We manage quite well.'

He didn't seem to hear her and talked over her.

'I propose to leave everything I possess to John with the proviso you add the name Allen to his name, calling him John Burnett-Allen.'

He fell back heavily in his chair, his strength sapped.

Hannah's head reeled with shock, first from discovering Edward was her real father and second, he was making John his heir. Her legs throbbed and she clutched the arm of the chair for support. With an effort, Edward pulled himself to the edge of his chair, reaching out to touch her hand. Shuddering at the cold, clammy touch she stared at him.

'Please, Hannah, I haven't long to

live. For the boy's sake, I implore you to recognise the fact he is my grandson. I want to make it legal.'

He fumbled in the breast pocket of his waistcoat and withdrew a small, square, leather case.

'You are my daughter. Please take this.'

She hesitated then accepted it.

'Open it,' he commanded.

She lifted the lid to reveal a miniature painted on ivory and gasped in amazement. The portrait of the woman could have been herself.

'Who is she?' she whispered.

'My mother, your grandmother.'

Wearily he sank back, closing his eyes.

'Why didn't my grandmother see me?' His voice was barely audible.

'Because I committed a mortal sin. I never acknowledged you as my daughter.'

Hannah remained very still. Somewhere in the house she could hear the children laughing and this aroused Edward.

'May I see John?'

No, was her first instinct. This man had made her and her siblings endure the régime of the orphanage, but she didn't want revenge. Her son had suffered the loss of his father and she couldn't deny him his grandfather, no matter what she thought of Edward Smith-Allen.

'Very well. Come up to the nursery.'

For the last few months of his life, Edward was a constant visitor to Arden Square and John, now a sturdy little boy, enjoyed the attention the old man lavished on him. They made each other laugh.

★   ★   ★

Since Robert's death, Tom visited Hannah every time he was home from sea, keeping her up to date with the rise of the fishing industry.

Sitting in Ruby's kitchen one day, enjoying tea, he remarked to Hannah, 'I see Christian Hansen's bought another smack. That's two he owns now. They say he's a hard taskmaster.'

After Tom had gone, Hannah sat thinking of Christian and during the days that followed, he was constantly in her thoughts. One day, walking to Hope House, she thought she saw him in the street.

'Christian,' she called, but the man turned and gave her a toothless grin.

After that, Hannah threw herself more and more into expanding Hope House, renting the property next door and turning it into a corner shop selling everything they made, from buns, meat pies and toffee apples to mufflers, caps, fishermen's socks and jerseys. Each evening she would arrive home exhausted, but happy to bath and play with the children.

She often wondered about going down to the dock to make enquiries about Christian's whereabouts, but then dismissed her idea as foolish. How could she, a respectable widow, think of doing such a thing?

9

A year later, Christian Hansen stood on the deck of the Indigo looking down the Humber into the setting sun. A wide canvas of sky held fleeting shades of flame red intermingled with swirls of burned orange.

He watched the first mate swing ashore to be greeted by his wife. Lucky man, he thought, having a wife.

But now he had a duty to perform, one he hated, to see Ned Watkins' wife and tell her Ned was dead. In a storm in the middle of the North Sea, Ned had caught his foot in a coil of rope and lost his balance. Christian had hung on to him but a mighty wave lashed over them both, knocking Christian out. When he regained consciousness, Ned had disappeared overboard. Christian felt sick. This had been his first fatality.

On the quayside, he passed travellers

from the Baltic countries who were en route to the new country of opportunity, America. Feeling low in spirit, he found himself wondering what kept him here in Kingston-upon-Hull when he could easily pull up his fragile roots and go to America. Perhaps it wasn't such a bad idea to sell up and cross the Atlantic Ocean. His fleet of four fishing smacks and the new house he'd bought in the fashionable area west of the dock would fetch a tidy profit.

Later that same afternoon, Hannah was sitting in the tiny office in Hope House doing the weekly accounts when she heard the raised voice of Amy outside in the passage.

'No, you can't see her. Come back on Monday.'

Hannah pushed back the ledger and went to investigate.

'What's the . . . '

She stopped sharp. In the narrow passageway stood Christian Hansen, with a boy of about three in his arms. Her heart did a quick leap and she clutched at the door to steady herself.

'I've told him,' Amy began.

'Amy, dear, I'd love a cup of tea and one for Skipper Hansen and milk for the boy.'

She smiled at Christian.

'Please, come into the office.'

Christian's big frame filled the tiny office. Conscious of his nearness and the fresh tang of the sea on his clothes, she felt herself trembling.

'You look well, Hannah,' he said, his voice deep, sensual.

'So do you,' she replied, but looking closer she saw beneath his rugged, tanned face deep lines were etched, and he was leaner. Then realising she was staring, she spoke briskly.

'How can I help?'

'Jimmy's dad was lost overboard and his mam is poorly. Neighbours are looking after her, but I need someone to look after this little chap for a short time. I can pay for his keep. Would you help me, Hannah?'

His eyes held hers.

Without hesitation she replied, 'Of course, I can. Leave him with me.'

He refused tea.

'I must get back to the smack, but I'll be back tomorrow.'

She was about to say they didn't open Sunday, but stopped herself. Watching him walk away, she noticed he was limping.

She took Jimmy home with her and bathed him with her children then gave him supper. They were naturally curious about the boy, who appeared quite timid and Charlotte, bless her, decided to mother him.

Next morning Hannah left the house before anyone stirred and went to Hope House. There she busied herself. After finishing the accounts, she wandered from room to room. It was very quiet. Amy was staying with friends and wouldn't be back until Monday.

In the workroom, she sorted through some old clothes and was snipping off buttons when the door opened, and there stood Christian. She looked at him, not sure what to say, feeling like a young, tongue-tied girl instead of a woman of twenty-five. She watched as he walked around the room looking at the work in progress on the benches. Then he turned to her.

'I had no idea that Hope House was so industrious. Who funds it?'

'We are self-sufficient,' she exclaimed proudly. 'Though we did have help at first.'

'Hannah, you are a marvel.'

'Come through into the kitchen and I'll make a pot of tea.'

'Where is everyone?'

'It's Sunday, our day of rest.'

'You came especially for me?'

She nodded and quickly went to the cupboard to take out cups and saucers. By the time they sat down at the scrubbed, wooden table for their refreshment, she began to feel less inhibited and more relaxed.

They reminisced of the time when Christian lived with the family in Fretter's Court.

'Your mam was a lovely woman. She knitted my first pair of sea-socks, you know.'

Suddenly the conversation stopped and they both fell silent. Hannah stared into her empty cup thinking of her old neighbour, Mrs Skinner, who used to read tea leaves. What did the future hold for her?

On impulse, she said, 'Come home with me and see Jimmy. Stay for Sunday roast. Ruby always does us proud.'

As they walked side by side she was again conscious of his limp, and curious, she asked, 'Did you have an accident?'

'Aye, I took a bashing in a storm.'

His eyes clouded as he thought of Ned in his watery grave.

'My goodness!' Ruby exclaimed on seeing Christian. 'I thought you'd left town long ago.'

'I'm thinking of it.'

Hannah shot him a quick glance but he didn't enlighten them further. Her heart gave a funny lurch.

They all sat down to eat in the dining-room, the only day the room was used now. Jenny's young man, Alfred, was also invited and today Fanny was in charge of the children. They had eaten earlier and Christian promised to take them all down to the pier later in the afternoon.

Ruby bustled about, declaring, 'It's nice to see men at the table.'

She promptly set the roast joint of lamb in front of Christian for carving. He looked to Hannah for approval. She nodded her consent. Watching him doing this simple act, she thought she never dreamed it could ever be possible to be sharing a meal with the man she loved. She sighed inwardly, curbing her desire to jump up and fling her arms about him.

The meal passed pleasantly. Alfred was eager to learn all about fishing, much to Jenny's dismay.

'When are you sailing, Skipper?'

Christian looked thoughtful before answering.

'I'm taking this trip off. I've a good first mate who can act as skipper for one trip.'

Alfred looked disappointed with the answer and turned his attention back to Jenny. Hannah could not help wondering if Christian's intention to miss a trip was connected to his earlier remark, that he was considering leaving Kingston-upon-Hull.

Later, with three excited children skipping ahead, Hannah walked by Christian's side as they made their way along Queen Street to the pier.

'You are very quiet, Hannah,' he exclaimed.

'I was thinking how nice to be walking out on a Sunday afternoon, just like a real family,' she said wistfully.

'Is that important to you?'

'Yes,' she answered simply, 'it is.'

Tears pricked her eyes.

'You are lonely, Hannah?'

She didn't meet his eyes.

'I have the children and my work at Hope House.'

Just then, John tripped on the uneven pavement and tumbled. Hannah rushed to scoop him up, but he said indignantly, 'Put me down, Mama. I'm a big boy now.'

Reluctantly she let him go, longing to feel the comfort of his tender body in her arms. On reaching the pier, they all stood near the iron railings overlooking the river. It was a bright, clear day and the banks of Lincolnshire were visible across the other side.

'Look, Mama,' Charlotte said, pointing to a dot moving down the Humber.

'It's one of mine,' Christian exclaimed proudly. 'Would you like to go to the dock and watch it berth?'

'Yes, yes,' the children chorused.

Over the children's heads Christian's and Hannah's eyes met and she smiled her approval.

The familiar smells of the dock were welcoming and Hannah felt at ease. Charlotte and John were excited at their first visit, which rubbed off on Jimmy. Hannah made a mental note to visit

Jimmy's mother.

As they waited on the quayside, a passing fisherman called to Christian.

'Hear you're thinking of selling up and going to America.'

Hannah held her body rigid, waiting for his reply.

'Only a rumour,' he replied then he turned to Hannah. 'You wouldn't want me to leave?'

She spoke quietly but firmly.

'I never want you to go, Christian.'

He slipped his hand into hers, gazing adoringly into her face.

'I love you, Hannah. I always have.'

'I love you, too, Christian,' she replied, leaning against him.

'Enough to marry a fisherman?'

'Yes. The sea is part of my life.'

'United, we will be strong, yah?'

She stood on tiptoe and kissed him.

'It's here,' John called as the smack came smoothly into berth.

Hannah watched Christian stride to his boat, a tall, powerful man, and her heart brimmed with love. She wasn't going to pretend it would be easy married to a fisherman. The sea could be cruel and unpredictable, but together they would survive. To have and to hold, from this day forth — a good motto, she thought as she moved to stand by Christian's side.

THE END

We do hope that you have enjoyed reading this large print book.

Did you know that all of our titles are available for purchase?

We publish a wide range of high quality large print books including:
Romances, Mysteries, Classics
General Fiction
Non Fiction and Westerns

Special interest titles available in large print are:
The Little Oxford Dictionary
Music Book, Song Book
Hymn Book, Service Book

Also available from us courtesy of Oxford University Press:
Young Readers' Dictionary
(large print edition)
Young Readers' Thesaurus
(large print edition)

For further information or a free brochure, please contact us at:
Ulverscroft Large Print Books Ltd.,
The Green, Bradgate Road, Anstey,
Leicester, LE7 7FU, England.
Tel: (00 44) **0116 236 4325**
Fax: (00 44) **0116 234 0205**